Praise for
LINDSAY McKENNA

"An absorbing debut for the Nocturne line."
—*Romantic Times BOOKreviews* on *Unforgiven*

"Ms. McKenna brings readers along for a fabulous odyssey in which complex characters experience the danger, passion and beauty of the mystical jungle."
—*Romantic Times BOOKreviews* on
Man of Passion

"Lindsay McKenna will have you flying with the daring and deadly women pilots who risk their lives…buckle in for the ride of your life."
—*WritersUnlimited* on *Heart of Stone*

Praise for
SUSAN GRANT

"A gripping, sexy new series!
I could *not* put it down!"
—*New York Times* bestselling author
Gena Showalter on *Moonstruck*

"For readers who want strong heroines and sexy alien hunks, [Susan Grant] is definitely still the go-to author."
—*The Romance Reader* on
How to Lose an Extraterrestrial in 10 Days

"Susan Grant writes heroes to die for!"
—*USA TODAY* bestselling author Susan Kearney
on *My Favorite Earthling*

LINDSAY McKENNA

As a writer, Lindsay McKenna feels that telling a story is a way to share what and how she sees the world that she lives in. Love is the greatest healer of all, and the books she creates are parables that underline this belief. Working with flower essences, another gentle healer, she devotes part of her life to the world of Nature to help ease people's suffering. She knows that the right words can heal and that creation of a story can be cathartic in a person's life. She hopes that her books may educate and lift the reader in a positive manner. Lindsay can be reached at www.lindsaymckenna.com or www.medicinegarden.com.

SUSAN GRANT

RITA® Award winner and *New York Times* bestselling author Susan Grant loves writing about what she knows: flying, adventure and the often unpredictable interaction between men and women! When she's not writing romances set in far-flung locales, Susan pilots 747 jumbo jets to China, Australia, Europe and many other exotic overseas destinations where she finds plenty of material for her novels.

LINDSAY McKENNA

SUSAN GRANT

Mission: Christmas

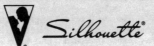

Romantic
SUSPENSE

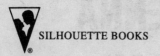 SILHOUETTE BOOKS

ISBN-13: 978-0-373-27605-9
ISBN-10:   0-373-27605-2

MISSION: CHRISTMAS

Copyright © 2008 by Harlequin Books S.A.

The publisher acknowledges the copyright holder
of the individual works as follows:

THE CHRISTMAS WILD BUNCH
Copyright © 2008 by Lindsay McKenna

SNOWBOUND WITH A PRINCE
Copyright © 2008 by Susan Grant

Visit Silhouette Books at www.eHarlequin.com

Printed in U.S.A.

CONTENTS

Dear Reader,

On these brisk November nights, what better way to keep warm than to get caught up in suspenseful romances by two of the most popular writers in the biz? You'll adore *Mission: Christmas* (#1535), with heart-warming stories from *USA TODAY* bestselling author Lindsay McKenna and *New York Times* bestseller Susan Grant. Both of these gals have lived it, loved it and are bringing their holiday wishes to you.

To further enrich your season, don't miss Linda Conrad's *The Sheriff's Amnesiac Bride* (#1536), the latest installment in our miniseries, THE COLTONS: FAMILY FIRST. A sheriff stumbles upon a pregnant beauty who doesn't remember where she came from and why she's in danger. Loreth Anne White brings us a brand-new miniseries, WILD COUNTRY, with the sexy and harrowing *Manhunter* (#1537). While trying to outsmart a serial killer, a lawman must protect the woman he loves. You'll enjoy the second book in Gail Barrett's miniseries, THE CRUSADERS, *To Protect a Princess* (#1538), where an adventurous hero saves a royal from a vicious threat.

As always, we deliver on our promise of breathtaking romance set against a backdrop of suspense. Have a wonderful November and happy reading!

Sincerely,

Patience Smith
Senior Editor

THE CHRISTMAS WILD BUNCH

Lindsay McKenna

To my brother, Gary Gent, who served in Vietnam.
Thank you for your service to all of us.

Chapter 1

"They're called the Wild Bunch, Major Klein," Agent Carl Bennington warned. He pushed his glasses up on his hawklike nose and watched her through narrowed eyes. "You've been assigned to the Nogales Border Patrol unit, and we're glad to have you aboard. The Black Jaguar Squadron down in Peru was also known as a wild bunch. That's why I wanted you here with us. I need a wild woman to tame a bunch of wild men. Your credentials precede you."

Dallas Klein sat in the straight-backed chair in front of the commander's oak desk, which was scattered with reports. "Sir, we cracked the mold on Apache pilots. We proved females could handle the big combat helos, in our work interdicting drug shipments out of Peru. We stopped tons of cocaine from coming to the shores of North America. The BJS continues to be a viable force against the drug trade to this day. Major Maya Stevenson, our company commander, pushed the limits by insisting that an all-female cadre could carry out these dangerous missions. In the six years I served as executive officer to the BJS, our numbers have been impressive."

Bennington nodded and looked down at his papers. "Major, when I saw your stats, I begged the powers that be to get you up here to help us. Frankly, I don't care if you're an alien from another planet and green in color." He punched his blunt finger down on the desk. "You ladies know interdiction like few in our trade do. I was impressed as hell by your moxie, your strategies and tactics to stop the flights."

Feeling a rush of pride, Dallas smiled. "It's nice to be praised for what we did as a company of women, sir. And I'm glad to know that you're gender blind."

Grunting, Bennington nodded and ran his fingers through his thinning hair. "Well, I'm not doing you any favors, Major Klein. Are you familiar with what's been going on along our border with Mexico since 9/11? I know you were in Peru at the time, and I don't expect you to be up-to-date."

"The shift in the drug flow? Yes, I'm aware." Dallas appraised her new C.O. He had to be in his fifties, and was dressed casually in a short-sleeved white shirt and tan Dockers. His cramped, air-conditioned office here in Nogales, Arizona, very close to the border, reminded her of Major Stevenson's office—messy. Dallas's own office was always the epitome of tidiness. That was her forte: bringing organization to chaos.

"Yes, the routes have changed dramatically. I've been in charge of border interdiction for the state of Sonora, just across from us, for a while now." He pointed to the window, where, through the slats of the venetian blinds, Dallas could see the sun beginning to rise over the dusty desert. "This drug running to the U.S. border is the brainchild of Manuel Navarro, the head of the Colombian drug ring. He's the guy that bought the Kamov helicopters from Russia, and is using them in South America to protect his trade routes and operations. I'm sure you're familiar with Navarro and his Kamovs."

"Very familiar," Dallas said grimly. "We've had a lot of sky combat with those bastards. So far, it's a draw. But Navarro is a greedy kingpin who wants to expand his empire. I figured he'd turn north and try to include Mexico in some way."

"Navarro is creative, if nothing else," Bennington agreed. "And he favors air transport of drugs. He couldn't use the Russian helos up here, so he switched to the Cessna workhorse, the C-206 Stationair."

"So the reason you wanted me is because of my drug interdiction experience down in South America?" All Dallas had seen since she'd arrived in Nogales was a lot of cactus, chaparral and endless desert. This landscape was barren compared to the hot, humid jungle where she'd lived for the last six years. A complete change. But then, she had been born in Tel Aviv, and her country was desert. This was more like home, and that made her feel good. She had recently visited Israel for a month, spent a wonderful time with her parents, who worked for the Mossad. Now she was back on loan to the U.S. government, as before, and Dallas relished her global role in stopping drugs.

"That's exactly why I asked for you. If anyone knows Navarro, Major, you do. You can help us stop these incoming drug shipments." Bennington got up and poured more coffee into his mug. He held up the pot. "More, Major Klein?"

Rising, Dallas offered her cup and kept it steady as he filled it. "Thank you, sir."

With a grunt, Bennington settled in his squeaky leather chair once more. He glanced over the rim of his glasses. "May I be frank with you, Major Klein?"

Sitting in turn, Dallas sipped her coffee. "Always, sir. If I'm to be the X.O. of your operation, there *has* to be honesty between us." When Bennington smiled, she saw that his front teeth were slightly crooked. The knowing smile reminded her of a coyote.

"That's what I want to hear. While we're alone, I'm Carl, and I'm calling you Sarah."

"Although Sarah is my given name, sir, I prefer to be called Dallas."

"A nickname?" Bennington asked.

"Of sorts." Shifting in her seat, Dallas set her mug on the edge of his desk. "As a child growing up in Israel, I had a love affair with the American Wild West. My parents read me a book about the cowboys of Dallas and Fort Worth, Texas, and at the tender age of three, I demanded to be called Dallas. I wanted to be one of those cowboys." She grinned.

"I see this as a good sign," Carl told her with a chuckle. "Okay, Dallas it is. You and I will work as a team. The C.O. and X.O. are inseparable, and you know from experience I'm the good cop, and you're the bad cop. X.O.'s always handle the mess in a squadron or company."

"I'm well aware of that role, yes, sir."

Frowning, Bennington straightened. "I'm going to be blunt, Dallas. I've got a personnel problem here in my squadron. And the last X.O. couldn't or didn't want to handle it, which is why I jettisoned him. Maybe what I need in order to tame the Wild Bunch is a woman, not a man."

"Good discipline shouldn't hinge on gender, Carl," she parried. "If it's a personnel problem, why can't you discharge the troublemaker?"

"The Wild Bunch is composed of three men, all ATF agents. The problem is they're damn good at what they do and are some of the smartest and gutsiest pilots I've got. I don't want to lose them. But I sure as hell don't want them behaving like cowboys. They break a lot of rules and regs to get the job done. I'm afraid that if these three men are allowed to continue without a firm hand, they're going to sink to the level of the smugglers we're trying to stop."

"I see," Dallas murmured. "So it's just as you said—a wild woman to tame a wild bunch."

Carl chuckled. "Sort of, but your record is impressive and impeccable. You helped to create the BJS without any blueprint, without any help from our government. And you did it successfully. I believe you have exactly what it takes to manhandle these three rogue pilots of mine. Otherwise, I'm going to have to get rid of them, and that would be a terrible loss. In particular, Agent Mike Murdoch has helped shape how we hunt and halt the air-to-ground smuggling originating out of the state of Sonora. He and his buddies just need, well, I'm hoping, a woman's touch to bring them around."

"What was your last X.O. like?"

"Agent Bailey Turner was a hard-nosed and by-the-book kind of man. He was an ex-Army pilot, and had spent a lot of time in Afghanistan before joining the ATF five years ago."

"You're saying his management style didn't put a dent in the Wild Bunch's antics and behavior."

Giving her an admiring look, Carl said, "I'm impressed with your immediate grasp of the situation."

Dallas felt another inner glow at his praise. "I often find it more useful to ask questions than give orders. Your three ATF agents are obviously a talented and skilled group. My instinct would be to work with them and observe, until I understand what's going right and what needs reshaping."

With a sigh, Carl sat back in his chair. "You're a godsend, Dallas. Your management style will be just what the Wild Bunch needs."

Dallas heard the unmistakable sound of two small planes landing on the asphalt runway nearby. As she peered out the window, she saw a Cessna turbo Stationair 206 flash by. In her new assignment, this tough workhorse plane would be her home,

instead of an Apache helicopter. Fortunately for her, she was
licensed to fly fixed wing aircraft as well as helicopters. Dallas
was sure it was one of the reasons she'd got this job.

"Ah, the Wild Bunch is back. Good." Bennington gave her
a searching look. "Murdoch is the head of the group. Everyone
looks to him. He's a rebel with a cause. Unfortunately, he just
went through a nasty divorce, and I know he's not feeling
kindly toward women right now. Be prepared, Dallas. I'm
hoping he won't drop a load of prejudice your way, but you
never know."

"Forewarned is forearmed," Dallas answered. "May I go introduce myself to the men?"

"Let's meet them at the reporting area. They're supposed to
file their flight reports at ops, and then we can talk with them.
That's a good place to introduce you as my new X.O. and the
fact I'm making you the fourth member of their group." Rising,
Bennington pulled his dark blue ATF cap onto his head. "Come
on, Dallas. Time to meet the Wild Bunch."

Mike Murdoch had just finished scribbling his signature on
a report when the door to their small ops room opened. Brilliant
morning sunlight slanted into the space where he and the other
two pilots sat. After recognizing Bennington's lean, wolflike
frame, he turned to the person standing behind him. Since the
X.O. had left a month ago, Murdoch figured it was his new boss.
The light was so bright he couldn't make out any details yet. Unhappily, he glanced at Jake Gardner and Bob Howard, who were
still working on their reports at the large rectangular table.
Scraping his chair loudly across the hardwood floor, he stood.

"Agent Bennington?" he said in a growl. Usually, their C.O.
hid behind his desk in his office, a fact that made Mike happy as
hell. The less the head ATF agent messed with them, the better.

"At ease, everyone," Bennington said, and stepped aside.

"This is our new executive officer, Major Dallas Klein. Major Klein, let me introduce you to our pilots."

Murdoch stared in surprise. The tall, slim woman in the green flight suit blew him away. A woman? Impossible! They'd ridden roughshod over the last X.O. just to get the bastard to leave them alone so they could do what they did best—finding and downing drug smugglers. But...a woman? Mike scowled as he took a good look at her, noting at once how confident she seemed, her shoulders thrown back with pride. She had an oval face with olive skin, and her sable-colored hair barely brushed the collar of her flight suit. Mouth tightening, he tried to ignore his body's response to this very attractive woman.

Meeting and holding her unusual golden eyes, Mike realized she was different, not a type he'd ever run into before. Oh, there were women ATF agents, for sure, but not in their game, and certainly not cowboys riding the border to flush out drug smugglers. He saw an alertness in Klein's gaze that made him uncomfortable, as if he were staring into the eyes of a golden eagle—eyes that missed nothing.

"Major Klein, let me introduce you to our men," Bennington said. "Agent Mike Murdoch has been with this border unit for two years."

Dallas felt a riffle of danger as she stepped forward and offered her hand to the scowling agent. He was in his early thirties, she guessed, as she gazed into the glacial blue eyes trained on her. There was no welcome in his square face, his thinned mouth. Tension radiated from his body, which had to be six feet tall. Still, Dallas found his craggy face handsome, even shadowed as it was by a five o'clock beard. His green flight suit showed off his powerful male body, the sleeves carelessly rolled up to just below his elbows.

"Agent Murdoch," Dallas said, stepping forward and thrusting out her hand. She deliberately maintained eye contact, and by the way he tensed his hard jaw and flashed her a steely look of competition, she knew she would have her hands full dealing with him. She saw his gaze flit from her face to her proffered hand, obviously weighing whether to shake it or not. Not to do so would be a flagrant sign of disrespect.

Dallas waited. She wasn't about to take no for an answer from this pilot. A few strands of his short, black hair fell across his furrowed brow, giving him a boyish look. Where was the boy within him? Dallas wondered. Could she reach that hidden side of him, instead of the cold male who clearly didn't want her to step into his world?

"My hand is getting tired, Agent Murdoch," she said with a slight smile, hoping to break the ice.

He thrust his arm forward. Surprised at the warmth and firmness of her handshake, he jerked his hand away, as if burned. "Major Klein, welcome to the Wild Bunch," he muttered, though he knew he didn't sound the least bit sincere. Slanting a glance to his left, where Jake and Bob sat, he saw their jaws had dropped over the fact that a woman was going to be their X.O.

"Thank you, Agent Murdoch." Dallas turned, and as her boss introduced the other two pilots, they shook her hand promptly.

Bennington smiled quizzically. "This morning you'll give Major Klein your reports on the activity you encountered. She needs to get her feet wet." Then he looked squarely at Mike, whose scowl was deepening by the second. "Murdoch, you'll no longer be flying solo. I'm assigning Major Klein to team with you." He glanced at the other pilots. "Jake and Bob will continue to fly together. ATF regs require a pilot and copilot on our missions, so Major Klein's involvement will bring us up to speed. As soon as she's steeped in your drug interdiction routines, and trained up through your experience, she'll take over strategy and tactics on missions."

"Yes, sir," Mike said gruffly.

Dallas felt the rage churning in Murdoch as he snarled out the words. Bennington didn't react, nor did she. Okay, he'd thrown down the gauntlet, judging from the look in his icy blue stare. Dallas got the message and the challenge. The flash in his slitted gaze was enough to chill anyone. She wouldn't call it hatred, but damn close. Girding herself internally, she told Bennington, "Thank you, sir. I think we'll work things out between us." She eyed the other two seemingly less hostile pilots. Jake and Bob appeared more stunned than angry. That was fine. She would use her gender as a way to open up a positive front with them.

"Excellent. I'll see you later, Major." Bennington excused himself.

Jake and Bob quickly scrambled to their feet. They both made excuses and hastily left the office. Dallas felt the coming confrontation with Murdoch. His shoulders were tensed, his hands clenched at his sides. But she wasn't about to let him walk all over her.

Once the door closed, she held his glare. "Let's sit down, Mr. Murdoch. I've got a lot to learn, and Agent Bennington said you were the go-to person." She pulled back a chair near where he had been sitting. "Shall we get to it? I'll only take about an hour of your time, because I know you've been out flying for five hours and you must be tired."

Puzzled, Mike jerked back the chair at the end of the table. Whatever he'd expected, it wasn't this. Her voice was husky and warm at the same time. She'd just given him an order, yet framed it in such a way that he couldn't take umbrage. He sat down and tried to disregard her beauty. Right now, he felt like a dog circling a cat, wary and distrustful. Who was she? And what kind of background did she have to be an X.O. in an elite operation like theirs?

"Can you fill me in on this latest flight?" Dallas asked, folding her hands on the table and holding his gaze. She saw shock mixed with confusion in the depths of his blue eyes. Good. That's where Dallas wanted him. Still, he was ruggedly handsome, with those rebellious strands of black hair falling across his broad brow. So much about him called to her on a feminine level.

Dallas hid her reaction to Murdoch, who epitomized the American cowboy. There was a swagger in his stride, a weathered look to his darkly tanned face. And if she was honest with herself, she'd have to admit she was drawn to his firm mouth, tight with emotion. She liked the shape of it, how the upper lip was slightly thinner than the lower one. His nose was lean and aquiline, reminding her of the profile of a Roman general on an old coin. Yes, there was a lot to like about Murdoch in the looks department, but Dallas knew better than to go there. She had to work with this guy and needed to gain his confidence. Could she?

Mike grabbed a map of the Sonoran desert area and threw it on the table before her. "I don't expect you know anything about this type of operation," he began in a gravelly tone as he spread it flat. "This is the real Wild West, Major. We're the good guys, trying to stop all the Latinos trying to bring marijuana, cocaine and heroin across our border. They'll use any isolated airstrip they can find as a place to unload their drugs." Jabbing at one section with his finger, he said, "This is the Vicente Guerro area, about fifty miles south of Nogales in the Sonoran mountains. It's a real hotbed of activity right now, because me and my friends have been flying to the west, near Altar, and forcing them to this new region. The Mexican pilots fly Cessna Stationairs, same as we do, what we call C-206s. They're an ideal aircraft for the terrain, able to navigate short landing strips in the middle of nowhere, and still carry huge loads of drugs. Recently, we interdicted 836 pounds of marijuana at that strip. We flew our own 206s in at dawn and caught the bastards on the ground, just loading up."

Hearing the satisfaction in his tone, Dallas nodded. "That's excellent, Agent Murdoch."

Not expecting praise, much less understanding from the new

X.O., Mike stared at her. She was only three feet away, and he could smell the scent of roses. Was it her perfume? Or maybe the shampoo she used on her shiny, dark brown hair. He hated that he even noticed. Hated even more that he was affected by her. "Do you have any idea what this type of operation entails?" he growled, shooting her a dark glance. He wanted to put her in her place, manipulate her into being a quiet mouse in the corner when their team decided on tactics and strategy.

As she examined the map, Dallas saw a lot of red dots scattered across the mountainous regions of Sonora. "Are the dots landing strips?" she asked, disregarding his question completely.

Frowning, Mike said, "Yes, they are." Okay, maybe he'd underestimated her alertness. But no woman could possibly know what danger they faced daily, or manage the crazy flying they did as they chased these hombres.

"The Turbo Cessna 206 needs 835 feet to take off in," she said, pointing to the topo map. "Its service ceiling is 27,000 feet, so the druggies can use strips in the valleys or high deserts to their advantage. But with that type of ceiling, they can use mountain strips as well." She traced a line of dots with her index finger. "From my experience in Peru, I know the druggies like to take off from such areas, fly low and fast, below radar range. Down there, once they made it into Bolivian airspace, they would land at similar dirt strips, to off-load their bales to awaiting trucks, or other aircraft that would take them out of South America."

Sitting down, Murdoch stared at her. "You flew drug flights in South America?" Shock ran through him. She was too attractive, too clean, her flight uniform too pressed and neat, to do that kind of grungy, dangerous work.

"Yes, I did, Mr. Murdoch. I was part of a U.S. Army black ops for six years down there."

She noted his stunned expression. *Good.* Dallas wanted Murdoch to be properly impressed by her knowledge, which she felt was equal to his own. She was going to turn the tables on him, gently but firmly.

Glancing again at the map, she tapped it. "I never dealt with smugglers in a desert, just jungle conditions. My teammates and I flew Apache helos. We learned where new airstrips were being hacked out of the jungle, by flying daily reconnoitering ops to locate them. We also had the use of satellite intel. We'd be in the air before dawn, because most of the druggies flew C-206s that lacked the radar needed to avoid hitting mountains. They flew daylight hours only. During my years of service, our unit was responsible for stopping over a million pounds of cocaine from leaving Peru. We worked with the Peruvian government, the CIA and other intel organizations to accomplish our goals."

Mike gulped. When Major Klein lifted her head and met his stare, he saw her full lips pull into a slight smile. It was the glitter in her eyes that made him realize she was no stranger to the game of drug running. "I didn't know."

"Of course not. We were black ops. We still are. I just transferred out of there to move on to this assignment."

His new X.O. could have poured salt into his wounds, and she didn't. But he could never trust her. She was a woman, dammit. And after his divorce, he didn't want anything to do with women.

Yet Major Dallas Klein was going to be his boss. What the hell was he going to do?

Chapter 2

The September dawn was cool in the Sonoran desert. Girding herself, Dallas carried her flight bag across the tarmac of the airstrip, an M16 rifle across her shoulder. Parked just ahead of her was the tan-and-white Cessna 206 Stationair she would fly. This was her first day on the job, and she knew Murdoch would test her.

The sky to the east was pink, and she enjoyed the desert scenery, which reminded her of Israel. Dallas lamented that her month-long visit to Tel Aviv had gone by so quickly. She missed her parents already.

This latest assignment would be temporary. There was a new black ops forming for the Black Jaguar Squadron. Right now, it was in the planning stages at the Pentagon. Dallas had been alerted that she was up for consideration as the C.O. of the as-yet-unveiled project. Because the all-woman BJS had been so successful in Peru, the boys at the Pentagon had finally seen the light. They wanted to take the BJS model to other parts of the world, only with men added to the mix.

Still, it was going to be overseen and run by a woman—her—and that made Dallas feel good. At least the military was getting over its hissy fit about women pilots performing in combat. They could and did, as well as any man. In the meantime, Dallas wanted to stay active out in the field, until the important new ops assignment came together.

Tightening her grip on the handle of her duffel bag, she greeted the mechanic just opening the doors on the C-206.

"Morning to you, Major Klein," the man called, lifting his hand in a wave. "I'm Scotty, your mechanic." He flashed her a toothy smile, doffed his dark green Border Patrol cap and ran a hand through his thick, gray-streaked brown hair.

Smiling, Dallas walked over and shook his hand. "Thanks for the welcome, Scotty." The mandatory Kevlar bulletproof vests were sitting in the cockpit, she noted. She placed her duffel bag next to her vest on the copilot's seat. "Can you tell me where Agent Murdoch might be?" She glanced at her watch. "Take off is in ten minutes."

Chuckling, Scotty finished cleaning the cockpit Plexiglas and said, "Hey, the Wild Bunch parties hard and plays hard, Major." He raised his bushy brows. "I'm way past that kind of scene myself, but those rascals… Before Randy Grant got killed—he was Agent Murdoch's partner—those four dudes would take off for the nightclubs in Nogales as soon as they hit the tarmac and finished their reports. You would see them staggering back here the next morning, smelling of alcohol…."

His smile waned and his brown eyes grew serious as he walked back around the single-propeller Cessna to where she stood. "I'm a teetotaler now, and don't go for any of that, but the Wild Bunch does." Shrugging, he added, "They get the job done, despite everything."

"They come out here for a mission still *drunk?*" Dallas couldn't keep the alarm out of her voice.

The lean mechanic gave her a pained look. "This is your first day here, Major. Before you hang 'em, see what they do." He patted the fuselage of the C-206. "You've just signed on to a very dirty, dangerous business."

The cool breeze brought the sweet scent of broom snakeweed, a huge desert bush covered with tiny yellow flowers. Dallas looked around the quiet facility. A black-eared jackrabbit loped across the small airstrip and disappeared up a hill covered with the blooming plants. "I know it's dangerous, Scotty." Frowning, she asked, "How did Agent Murdoch's partner die?"

"It was pretty bad. Him and Mike tailed two C-206s flying near Los Mochis. They followed one down to what looked like a deserted dirt airstrip. When they went to arrest the pilot, smugglers hiding in a nearby hangar opened fire on them. Randy died in the firefight, but Mike got them all." Proudly, Scotty added, "Murdoch's a can-do kind of guy, Major. You want him at your back in a crunch 'cause he's fearless. Not only did he nail the druggies in the Cessna, he captured seven hundred pounds of marijuana, plus killed the three bad guys who were hiding in that hangar."

"How long ago did this happen?" Dallas began to wonder if Murdoch wasn't wrestling with grief over his partner's death. It would be normal to do so.

"A month ago." Scotty lowered his voice. "Major, he's had a bad run of luck of late. He just got finished with a nasty divorce. First, Randy dies, and then his ex-wife tore up his life. And now, well, you're his new partner." The mechanic eyed her wryly, and added, "You're a woman. He's not real keen on females right now, if you know what I mean. Not that any of this is your fault. You're the innocent walking into it."

Great. Dallas understood anyone dealing with the death of a loved one had a lot of grief to plow through. Her good friend Kat

Wallace, commander of a C-17 that delivered supplies to Lima for the Black Jaguar Squadron, had lost her brother last January. Mack Wallace had been a U.S. Marine serving in Iraq. Kat was not part of the all-female black ops of the BJS, but Dallas had struck up a friendship with the Air Force pilot. She had seen the thirty-year-old, baby-faced woman shut down emotionally after her brother's death.

Kat had started wearing her brother's dog tags during the last flights she'd made into Lima, before being reassigned to a unit in eastern Europe. It helped her ease her grief and stay connected to Mack, she'd told Dallas over shots of pisco, a powerful local drink in Peru. Seeing Kat suffer so badly, Dallas had ached for her friend.

As she sifted through those recent memories, she looked up to see a lone figure in a dark green flight suit making his way toward them. It was Mike Murdoch.

Okay, he was grieving, too. That was good to know. Further, with a fresh divorce making him emotionally raw, his hostile demeanor of yesterday could be understandable. He might not be angry at Dallas, but she was female, and therefore, the enemy. *Great. Just great.* It was hard enough fitting into a new squadron, but this made it doubly tough.

Dallas turned to Scotty, who was finishing up his ground duties around the Cessna. "Thanks for the info," she called softly. "I appreciate the heads-up."

He grinned. "You seem like a nice lady, Major. We're lucky to have someone of your caliber step in and fill the slot as Mike's partner. That dude needs a good, solid, steady person working with him. That's what Randy was, you know. He was always the cooler head that prevailed when things heated up, in the air and on the ground. Mike's the leader of the Wild Bunch for a reason." The mechanic flashed his uneven, toothy smile once more.

Nodding, Dallas wished she'd gotten this info from her commander. But then, life didn't work that way. The rank hierarchy often didn't know the facts of a situation unless someone like Scotty was around to let them in on the real story. "I owe you one," she called.

The mech gave her a shy smile. "Nah, you don't, Major. You just come back safe and sound. That's all I ask."

"That's my goal," she promised him.

The sun was barely peeking above the horizon when she turned back to Murdoch. He had his head down, his duffel bag slung over his one broad shoulder, M16 over the other, as he shuffled toward her. He was weaving slightly, and Dallas caught the odor of alcohol long before he arrived. And when he lifted his head, she noted his skin, bloodshot eyes and the thin set of his mouth. He was still drunk. *Damn.*

As he approached the C-206, Murdoch glowered at his new partner. Scotty said hello, and Mike merely grunted in answer. Why the hell did the major have to be so damn sexy? Dallas Klein made a rumpled, unisex flight suit look good. She was tall, and though she was slim, her full breasts and curving hips showed she was definitely female. Plus those long, long legs would be definitely worth exploring. Though unhappy with his libidinous reaction, he acknowledged the fact that the major was a damn fine-lookin' woman. Well, he was fried on women right now, and they were off-limits. So his reaction to this military pilot didn't make sense at all. But then, he was still drunk from a night of partying in Nogales.

He noticed Klein frowning at him. She had the most beautiful gold eyes he'd ever seen. They contrasted appealingly with her shoulder-length hair, which was caught up in a girlish ponytail. Her olive skin was so smooth, and that mouth of hers made his loins sizzle. Mike couldn't decide which was her best feature, those large, inquisitive eyes or those sinfully shaped full lips just begging to be kissed….

Mike seemed to come out of a fog as he saw her eyes narrow speculatively on him and her soft mouth purse. *Trouble*.

"Good morning, Agent Murdoch," Dallas said as he approached.

"Yeah, it is," he grunted. He started around the nose of his Cessna to take the pilot's seat.

"Hold it," she ordered.

Murdoch turned. *What the hell?* She was picking up her duffel bag from the copilot's seat and heading toward him. "What are you doing?" he groused. "You're my copilot."

"Not today, with the way you look and smell, Murdoch."

Shocked, Mike took a step back as she brushed by him. "What? Hey! Come back here, dammit!" He reached out, grabbed her upper arm and swung her toward him. What happened next, he wasn't expecting. The moment his fingers wrapped around her arm, she dropped her bag and turned swiftly. In seconds, Murdoch found himself flat on his back. Her knee was in the center of his chest, and she was scowling down at him.

"Don't *ever* grab me again, Murdoch. You won't live to talk about it with your buddies the second time around. Got it?"

Blinking twice, Mike stared up into her darkened eyes. What the hell had just happened? "Uh, yeah…"

Dallas removed her knee from his chest and stood back. She didn't offer to help him to his feet. The mechanic gave her a brief nod, as if to say she'd done the right thing under the circumstances.

"Now, Agent Murdoch, here's how things are going to go on this mission of ours this morning. I'm commander today. You're copilot. You're obviously hungover, still drunk. I can smell the alcohol from six feet away. You're my partner, and I'm not going to allow you to pilot a plane under these circumstances. Are we clear about our job assignments?"

Murdoch picked himself up off the tarmac, dusted off the rear of his flight suit and grudgingly reached for his duffel and rifle. "What the hell kind of move did you make on me?" he demanded, holding her furious stare.

"I'm Israeli, Agent Murdoch. I'm on loan to the U.S. government. Every Israeli soldier learns krav maga. It's how we protect ourselves."

Rubbing his stubbled jaw, he eyed her. "Yeah, I've heard of it. It's a nasty way to fight."

Giving him a brief, cutting smile, Dallas said, "It's a way to stay alive, Agent Murdoch."

"You're good."

"I have a black belt, the highest level in this style of fighting." Krav maga combined the best moves from different combat techniques and turned them into a lethal back-alley mix.

"Wouldn't you know it…" Murdoch muttered, finding new respect for her, as a woman and a soldier. "Damn good thing my ex-wife didn't know krav maga, or I'd be dead by now."

"Then don't ever make the mistake of thinking I'm her." The major pointed to her arm. "I'm off-limits to you, Agent Murdoch. You'd never have reached out and grabbed me if I were a man. So whatever rage you feel about your divorce and women, don't dump it on me. Got it?"

"Yeah, I got it." Smarting at her cool, husky tone, he watched her pick up her flight bag and head for the pilot's seat. Scotty said nothing, just stood in front of the Cessna, waiting for them to climb in and get harnessed up. After running his fingers through his hair, Mike changed direction and walked to the copilot's seat. Dallas was putting on the Kevlar vest near the open cockpit door. He threw his duffel in the back seat, after getting his revolver and tucking it in the leather holster beneath his right arm. Climbing in, he saw her glare at him. *Now what?*

"Mr. Murdoch, I'm assuming you forgot to put on your Kevlar vest because you're still drunk?"

He flinched beneath her warning voice and jerked the vest off the seat. "I don't ever fly with it," he snarled.

"You will with me. Put it on."

Anger swilled through Murdoch. His mind was still fogged with whiskey and he wasn't thinking clearly. "Dammit, I told you, I'm not flying with it on. It's too friggin' uncomfortable."

Fastening the Velcro straps of her chest armor, Dallas met his bloodshot eyes. He was acting like a pouty six-year-old. "Tell me, Agent Murdoch, was your last partner, Randy Grant, wearing his Kevlar vest when he died?"

Stung, Mike reared back. How did she know about Randy? And then he noticed Scotty's sheepish look. The mech had told her. Swinging his gaze back to her, Mike couldn't help but admire her in one way. But he sure as hell didn't want to take orders from any woman right now, X.O. or not. "Neither of us was wearing one at the time we nailed the bad guys."

"And if Randy had been wearing his vest, do you think he'd be standing here today instead of me?" Dallas slid her dark green flight helmet over her head and pushed up the visor.

Her low voice penetrated Murdoch's mounting anger, and he saw a flicker of compassion in her gold eyes. He realized belatedly that this woman really was a tour de force, certainly no office pogue who hadn't been around combat. Maybe that black ops down in Peru had given her the type of experience to see the truth of a situation. Rattled, he snarled, "Yes, Randy probably would be here. He took a slug to the chest."

Mike didn't have to finish the rest of the sentence. If he and his partner had worn their bulletproof vests, Randy would have survived that gunfight. Cursing softly, Mike reached behind the seat and jerked on the stiff garment. "There. Satisfied, Major?"

"I am now. Do the walk around, Agent Murdoch. That's what copilots do, unless you think you're above such an activity."

Mike's nostrils flared. Of course he knew the copilot always walked around the aircraft, looking for leaks, testing the propellers, wing flaps and rudders to make sure they were in working order. After the customary trip, he returned to his seat and climbed in. He let Klein know everything was in working order, and they got down to business. She was already harnessed in and waiting for him. No matter what way Mike looked at her—in profile or full-on—she was pretty.

As he fumbled with his harness array, Murdoch wondered if she was married. For sure, someone with her looks and body had to have a significant other. Grousing at himself, he shut the door and locked it. "Okay, I'm ready for preflight, Major." Normally, Mike didn't wear his flight helmet, either, but he figured he'd better this morning. He settled it on his head and donned his aviator sunglasses. His skull throbbed even more, but he remained silent. Where the hell had he put his aspirin?

Dallas handed him the preflight card. Moments later, they had finished with the short checklist, and she tucked it back in the net pouch beside her seat. She noticed Murdoch digging into his flight suit pockets, eventually pulling out a plastic Ziploc bag containing white tablets. Aspirin? She refrained from asking as he popped a couple into his mouth and washed them down with water.

Scotty removed the chocks from the nose wheel and then stood off to one side. He twirled his index finger in the air, which meant she could start the engine. In no time, Dallas had the C-206 idling. The whole plane shivered, and she applied rudders and throttle to take the Stationair out to the end of the short runway. A couple of jackrabbits raced across the asphalt in front of them.

"I had the opportunity last night to look over the Sonoran corridor, Agent Murdoch," she told him, fitting the mike close to her lips. "And today I want to make this mission count in two ways. First, I see that Santa Ana hasn't been checked out in the last three months. Your efforts have been focused in the western part of the state. Secondly, I need to acquaint myself with the

whole terrain, and that area is close enough. I don't want to undertake a real mission with you today, given the shape you're in."

Moving his mike to his lips, Murdoch spread the map across
his thighs. "Santa Ana is quiet. You're wasting our time."

"We'll see." Dallas anchored the small plane, pressed both
rudders to the floor and gently eased the throttle to takeoff speed.
In moments, the reving engine made the C-206 shake and shudder
as she held the craft in place. Releasing the rudders, which also
acted as brakes, Dallas smoothly eased the plane off the runway
and into the quiet morning air. As she got her bearings and banked
left toward the border, she told him, "Make the calls to the
Mexican officials that we're entering their airspace. I've already
filed a flight plan with them, and they should have it in hand."

"You're efficient," he grunted, adjusting the radio frequency
to report to the appropriate officials. Speaking in Spanish, he
gave their call sign, Wolf One, and let them know their latitude
and longitude. Then he switched the frequency back to their
Nogales unit, so they could be continuously monitored.

"I'm deeply disappointed in you, Agent Murdoch." Dallas
leveled off the plane at three thousand feet. Below them desert
stretched in every direction. To the south she could see the
purplish peaks of mountains washed by the rising sun. "Do you
fly drunk every day?"

"Dammit, get off my back, Major."

"Not a chance. I have to fly with you, Murdoch. How can I
trust you if we find druggies, have to land and go after them?
What part of your alcohol-drenched brain will be working? Right
now, I'm hoping there is no action in Santa Ana, because frankly,
you're a liability to me. You sure as hell can't protect my six."

"Okay, point taken." Murdoch was familiar with the term—
pilot lingo for the back or rear of something. In this case, she
referred to the fact he couldn't really protect her in a firefight. To
have someone's six meant being there to save that person's life.

That comment hurt. He'd already lost Randy, and he couldn't argue with her, either. He'd drunk more than he'd meant to last night. Realizing a woman would replace his best friend for four years was just too much for Mike to take. The whiskey had taken the sting out of the situation and given him a reprieve of sorts. Now, reality glared at him like a blinding light.

"It's more than a point," Dallas told him, holding his stare briefly. "You won't ever show up for a mission in this shape again. You got that, Murdoch? You and the Wild Bunch can party all you want, but you'd better arrive at work clean shaven, your hair combed—and not wearing yesterday's flight suit, which reeks of sweat."

The sun rose higher, and Dallas put on her dark aviator glasses. Anger raged through her, but as an X.O., she had to hold on to her feelings, say and do the right things. She noticed Murdoch had lost some of his gruffness and was looking pasty and hangdog. He said nothing, just picked up a pair of binoculars to scan the desert for druggies.

Her heart went out to him. To have lost his partner a month ago, and then finalize a divorce, the guy probably had lots of reason to get drunk. Still, Dallas wouldn't let that be an excuse. What they did for a living was dangerous, and Murdoch had to be a hundred percent when he flew with her.

Piloting the Cessna in the quiet air was a pleasure for Dallas. The sky was a light blue above the bright gold horizon. The half yoke used to guide this plane was a far cry from the cyclic and collective of the Apache helo she had flown almost daily in Peru. And this civilian airplane was a slug in comparison to that speedy military helicopter. But her mission was different. At least for a while, until her new Black Jaguar Squadron assignment came through.

"Hey," Mike called, suddenly sitting up straight. He'd been looking below, through the binoculars. "I think we got a bad guy at three o'clock, Major. It's a C-206 like ours, painted desert-brown so we can't see them all that well."

Tipping the wing slightly to the right, Dallas caught sight of the plane. "Good spotting," she exclaimed. Hearing the sudden excitement in Murdoch's voice, she grinned. "What's your next move when you spot a possible drug plane?"

"I'm calling the Mexican air channel people right now. If this guy has a flight plan, he's not a smuggler. The druggies never file flight plans." Mike jabbed a finger toward the fleeing plane. "He has no numbers on the sides of his fuselage, a dead giveaway that he's a smuggler. Still, we always check."

Pleased, Dallas dropped the plane down to one thousand feet. They were on the six, or rear, of the C-206, which was flying at about five hundred feet. Even if he was swiveling his head around, looking for them, the pilot would never see them at this angle. She gave a wolfish grin.

In no time, Murdoch had gone through the required steps. He sent Dallas a triumphant smile. "We got ourselves a druggie on the run."

"And Santa Ana is probably where he originated from, based on his flight trajectory."

"Yeah, you're right." Mike's assessment of her tactical abilities rose accordingly.

"What next? Do we force him down?" she demanded.

Surprised, Murdoch looked over at her. He saw her set profile. Right now, she was like a hawk intent on a victim. Gone was the soft, luscious mouth and the curvy, feminine woman. No, he was seeing an air combat warrior. "We have choices here, Major. We can call ahead and ask someone to force them down. Or we can do it. We can just follow the pilot until he lands at his intended airstrip, where he'll meet men planning to drive the bales across the U.S. border. What's your pleasure?"

"Let's force him down."

He liked the edgy excitement in her husky voice. She had both hands on the yoke and was within five hundred feet of the unsuspecting smuggler.

"You can fly up alongside him and gesture for him to land," Mike said, "or pull up to the pilot's side, and I'll poke the barrel of my M16 out the window here. I'll put a couple of shots right in front of his cockpit window. That is guaranteed to get his attention."

"What are the chances of them returning fire?" Dallas missed not having the missiles and rockets that were part of the Apache's vaunted arsenal. The Cessna was a civilian plane and had no armor, no weaponry.

"Depends," he said, twisting around and reaching for his rifle. With quick, knowing movements, he prepared to fire. "You never know."

"Good thing we have our vests on," she said, slanting a glance in his direction. She saw Murdoch smile sourly as he quickly and expertly readied the weapon. "Okay, I'm going to drop like a rock to his altitude and try to surprise him," Dallas warned. "You poke that rifle out the window, but don't fire. Just gesture for him to land."

"Are you always this nice, Major?"

Laughing, Dallas felt the adrenaline pump through her bloodstream. "I'm not known as nice to the druggies in Peru, Murdoch. They don't like to see me coming. Ready?"

"Yeah, let's go for it." Murdoch's brain was clearing, especially when he opened the window and fresh air started whistling through the cockpit. He stuck the barrel out the window. "Now," he told her gruffly, positioning himself.

Murdoch wasn't prepared for the swift, calculated movements she made with the plane. To say she was an adept pilot didn't quite cover it. She dropped the Cessna with a professionalism and swiftness that made him gasp. In seconds, Murdoch was staring at the surprised face of the Mexican pilot.

Dallas brought their aircraft within six feet of the smuggler's wing. The pilot's eyes went wide with shock and then panic. After gesturing for him to land, Murdoch put his hand on the trigger of the M16. The Mexican had a copilot, a younger man who reached back behind the seat. A revolver appeared in his hand.

"Dammit!" Murdoch snapped off several shots with his M16. The bullets ripped throughout the cockpit of the smuggler's plane, and suddenly, it swerved to the right and banked sharply.

Dallas followed in pursuit, the gravity tugging at her harness.

Smoke leaped up and out from beneath the fuselage cover. One of his bullets had struck the engine. "They're gonna try to make a run for it," Mike warned her. "Stay on them!"

"Like fleas on a dog," Dallas assured him grimly.

Murdoch was more than pleased with her flight capabilities. The druggies began to jink back and forth, so they couldn't get near enough to fire again. Both planes had descended to fifty feet above the desert floor. The air was rougher near the ground, for the risen sun was warming the soil and generating small updrafts. The smoke grew black and thick as it purled from the Cessna's engine.

"He's gonna have to land that sucker anywhere he can," Mike warned. "Back off a little. We'll let him put down and then follow him in. If he crashes, we don't want to be caught in the explosion or debris."

"Roger," Dallas said, lips thinned. Sure enough, she spotted a flat, gravelly spot just ahead among the lumpy hills. There was plenty of cactus and brush growing there, but Dallas knew a plane like this could land if it didn't run into anything with its tricycle gear.

"Back off more," Murdoch warned her. "The area they're heading for has a rough, dicey surface. We've seen planes flip over when a wheel catches a big piece of brush, and you don't want to be right behind them."

"Roger," she repeated.

The drug plane landed badly, then hopped back up into the air, plumes of dust flying around it. Then it hit the ground again. This time, the nose wheel plowed into a thicket of brush and collapsed. Dallas watched the craft skid, the propeller snapping off in pieces and disintegrating upon impact. The plane became enveloped in a huge, rolling cloud of dust as she landed their own Cessna, about four hundred feet away. The sand-gravel surface was solid in the stretch she'd chosen, thank goodness. Landing with a solid thump, she brought their plane to a quick stop by standing on the rudders, which acted like brakes for the aircraft. Before it stopped rolling, Murdoch bailed out the door, M16 in hand, and ran hell-bent-for-leather toward the crashed C-206 dead ahead of them. Smoke was pouring out of the smashed engine, and flames licked up here and there.

Why hadn't Murdoch waited? Dallas quickly stopped the plane, killed the engine and whipped off her harness. Before diving out the door, she grabbed her own M16, locking and loading it on the run as she sprinted toward the smugglers.

Dallas saw Murdoch a hundred feet ahead, circling toward the pilot's door. The Mexican kept hitting the jammed door with his boot until it finally yawned open, and he leaped out. Dressed in a pink shirt and jeans, he appeared to be no more than twenty years old. The kid from the copilot's seat quickly followed. He had a shaved head and also wore a white T-shirt and jeans. The two ran in different directions.

Murdoch fired several rounds into the air and yelled at them to stop. Both skidded to a halt, turned around with their arms high in the air.

By the time Dallas got to them, Murdoch had both men lying flat on their bellies, their arms stretched above their heads. He was looking pleased.

She grinned, sweat running from beneath her helmet and down her temples. "Good work," she praised.

"Thanks, boss." Murdoch motioned for her to go to the Cessna, the nose of which was buried in about two feet of sand and gravel. "Let's see what these dudes were carrying."

"Roger that." She turned and peeked in the open door. The smoke and flames of earlier were now out, so there was no worry the craft would explode. Climbing into the cabin, Dallas peered into the back of the plane. The smell of marijuana was overpowering. Taking a quick count, she eased out again and turned toward her partner. Murdoch had used nylon cuffs to bind the suspects' hands behind their backs and had them sitting on the ground when she walked up to him.

"Marijuana. Looks to be about ten bales. What does that mean in pounds?"

Murdoch gave a low whistle. "That's probably a max load for this plane. We'll get the contraband to the U.S. and weigh it, but I'd guess it will likely be around eight hundred pounds. Congratulations, Major. You've made a helluva bust on your first mission."

"Don't you think we can call each other by our first names when we're out here alone? Mine is Dallas." She thrust her hand forward, and he took it without hesitation.

"Mike. So long as you don't use any more of your krav maga on me, I'll call you Dallas." Murdoch squeezed her long, slim hand. She had a surprisingly firm grip. After all, he told himself, she was a black belt in combat, so why wouldn't she?

But as he gazed into her dancing golden eyes, he felt helpless to stop the sexual attraction he was feeling toward her. What a hell of a fix he was in.

Chapter 3

"**D**amn, it's cold," Dallas griped to Murdoch as they climbed into their intrepid Cessna. The November winds whipped past them, spitting rain—life-giving moisture that was always welcome in arid countries. The sky was slate-gray, with shreds of white stratus clouds hanging low on the horizon.

"Ah, you desert rats always have thin blood," Mike teased as he pressed the Velcro closed on his Kevlar vest and harnessed up. He noticed Scotty waiting patiently, chocks in hand. It was 6:00 a.m. and barely light. But that's when the bad guys took off, because they didn't have all the radar to fly at night.

Giving him a grin, Dallas settled her helmet on her head, strapped in and shut and locked the door. "Yeah, must be my Israeli blood showing. Israel is nothing but desert."

Mike handed her the preflight checklist and they quickly went through it. Everything was in order. When he took the list back from her, their fingertips met. Murdoch relished the chance to touch Dallas. Ever since he'd grabbed her on the tarmac and she'd thrown him to the ground with her krav maga techniques, he'd been both wary of and fascinated by her. It had taken two months for them to adjust to one another. They worked well together, like a team. But Mike couldn't help wishing for more contact. For now, he pushed the thought from his mind.

Dallas was pilot today. Since her first confrontation with Murdoch, he had cleaned up his act. He'd never again come on the tarmac drunk. He'd even stopped his hard drinking and partying in Nogales.

Dallas watched Scotty give her the signal, then she started up the engine. The Cessna coughed and sputtered.

"Even the plane is cold today," she remarked, listening to the motor catch and take hold. The prop whirled, and she eased off the rudders, letting the craft trundle to the end of its short runway, then turn around, ready for takeoff. Dallas paused there, waiting for a sudden rain shower to pass.

"Every plane has a personality," Mike agreed. "You want some coffee after we get airborne?"

"You bet."

He'd come to enjoy their intimate patter, their chance to be alone in the air. On the ground, Dallas was in charge. He couldn't be caught using such familiarity. But here in the air, their professionalism facade dissolved and they'd become like best buddies. Mike wanted more, but she seemed immune to his subtle suggestions. He'd sometimes touch her shoulder when they were teasing one another, or he'd crack a joke, and she'd laugh huskily in return. Whenever his fingers met hers, a pleasant ribbon of warmth flowed up his hand and arm.

The Cessna rolled down the runway after the squall had moved by. The aftermath of a hurricane that had started in Mexico on the Pacific side was making the skies dicey. In Arizona, the storm had already been downgraded to a low frontal system.

Once they leveled off at three thousand feet, the air was much less turbulent. Murdoch pulled out the large metal thermos from the net pocket, quickly poured Dallas half a cup of steaming black coffee and handed it to her. Another chance to touch the beautiful, remote Dallas Klein.

"Thanks," she said, gripping the metal cup. The warmth felt good to her fingers.

Mike dug into his net pouch for a second cup and poured himself some. Today, they were headed deep into Mexico, to Hermosillo. Mexican *federales* had located a secret airstrip outside the beautiful city, and the two of them were going to investigate. With a fading hurricane in the vicinity, rain would be falling off and on all day. It would do no good to hunt bad guys along the border because they would be grounded by the weather. Dallas had predicted that, and Mike agreed with her. The druggie action would come after the hurricane moved north. Right now, central Mexico enjoyed sunshine and clear blue skies, just the ticket for druggies to climb into their Cessna Stationairs, and Dallas hoped to intercept them. It was a solid tactical plan.

"Hey, how come I never see you with a dude?" Mike asked, keeping his tone light and bantering. Dallas grimaced and took another sip of her coffee. He had tried all kinds of ways to find out about the enigmatic woman's personal life but had failed. Yet was he really ready to hear she was in a relationship?

"Murdoch, you're a terrible tease."

Shrugging, he said, "Hey, you're not exactly an open book, you know. I'm just trying to find out if you have a relationship right now."

Chuckling, Dallas said, "My parents work for the Mossad. Did you expect me to be an open book? I grew up with two spies. They taught me well." She flashed him a grin.

Undeterred, Mike drawled, "Okay, fair enough, but I'm the guy that has your six. Can't you level with me?"

With a quizzical glance, she retorted, "Is it safe? You know, the first month you were a snarly dude. I was afraid you were going to bite my hand off."

Mike snorted. He couldn't help watching those luscious lips, curving sweetly upward in the corners. If he confided to Dallas he dreamed of her almost nightly, and mention what they did together in his dreams, she'd blush crimson and probably retreat even deeper into herself. "Listen, you're my X.O., and keeping things professional and detached are fine at the BP station. But this is me. I've changed. You can see that. You were right—I was snarly because of my divorce." He frowned. "And losing Randy, my partner." Dallas gave him a sympathetic look. "But stop feeling sorry for me, okay? I'd really like to know you personally."

"Hmm," Dallas murmured. "Why?"

"Because you're single, as far as I know, damn good-looking, and I'm a single guy myself." There, the truth was out. Mike wondered how she was going to handle it. Might as well find out.

Dallas finished her coffee and handed the cup back. "First of all, I am single. And no, I don't have a steady guy in my life right now."

"You used to?"

"Yes, back in Cuzco. He was a Peruvian medical doctor." Dallas shrugged. "Things got complicated. I was in a black ops, and he was a renowned heart surgeon. Between our two schedules, we rarely saw one another, and even then, if I got called back to BJS for an emergency, I was gone. His family put a lot of pressure on him to drop me, and eventually, he did."

"Families can do that," Mike agreed. He felt elated she was sharing with him. "Now, my family is very laid-back. I'm the oldest, with two younger sisters, Julie and JoAnn."

"Laid-back. Hmm. Like you, right?" Dallas chuckled.

Mike smiled back and scanned the gray sky and scudding clouds. Rain splattered across the cockpit window, but less and less frequently the farther south they flew. "I'm laid-back, too."

"Oh, right. Mr. Intense. You lock on to a druggie through your binoculars, and you're like a laser-fired rocket." She laughed wryly. "Give me a break, Murdoch. You're the least laid-back dude I've ever known, a bloodhound on a scent!"

"So, you don't like intense dudes? They're a turnoff? A surgeon isn't exactly a laid-back sort, either. They are well known type A personalities."

A smile lurked on her lips. "Murdoch, you're fishing. What's this all about?"

"Well…" he sighed, sitting back, sipping his coffee. "I wanted to invite you out to dinner tonight after we get back. I know a really nice Mexican couple in Nogales who've been friends of mine for years. I thought you might like to have some good home cooking, Mexican style. Since you spent six years in Peru, I thought you'd probably enjoy Latin food."

"Now that's a provocative invitation," Dallas said, trying to look serious. She noticed his black, straight brows moving downward. "Good food is always a draw for me."

"You mean you'd come along for the food? And not because you're with me?"

"You're incorrigible, Murdoch."

He grinned wolfishly and added, "Maria is a damn good cook. Her husband, Alfredo, is a businessman. He owns a trading post on both sides of the border. I think you'd enjoy them. They're very intelligent, compassionate people with big hearts. Did you know that at Christmas, they take thousands of dollars worth of gifts to orphanages in Sonora? Alfredo likes to dress up as Santa Claus, and Maria becomes Mrs. Claus. They're a hoot, the two of them."

"They sound like really nice people," Dallas said. "Yeah, I'd love to have dinner with them."

"How about with me?"

"Oh, Murdoch, will you stop?"

Feeling pleased, he decided not to push her anymore. Dallas

had colored prettily beneath his cajoling. She looked even more desirable with pink cheeks and that softness in her golden eyes. "I guess I can stop goading you," he said, "since you've agreed to have a date with me."

"It's not a date."

"What would you call it?"

"Just two friends having dinner with other friends."

"I guess I'll let you get away with that definition—for now."

Seeing her smile elated Murdoch as never before. He was curious. Why did Dallas refuse to call it a date? Was she drawn to him at all, or did she really see him as just a friend? That wasn't a status Murdoch wanted with her.

The plane bumped then leaped about fifty feet upward as it hit an air pocket. Dallas quickly stabilized it. She was a damn fine pilot, but so was he.

"You know," he said, putting the cap back on the thermos and getting down to business, "you and I have the best stats for October. We made five busts. Just think, about 4,500 pounds of marijuana and coke aren't gonna hit U.S. markets." He pressed his hand to his chest. "Does my heart good."

"Yeah, we are a good team," Dallas told him. "Better than I thought, given our rough landing when I first got here."

"That's over," Mike assured her. "I apologized. I had my nose bent out of joint over my divorce."

"I don't ever want to divorce. I want to fall in love and have it last forever. Maybe that's idealistic in a world where half the marriages crash and burn, but my parents are still married. That's what I want."

"Ahh, now I get it." Mike touched the center of his forehead and closed his eyes. "Great seer that I am, the reason why you want me only as a friend is you're afraid I'll dump you somewhere down the road, and you'll be alone with no hope of a forever marriage."

"Get real, dude!"

Chortling, Mike opened his eyes and shared her laughter. He loved the fact that every time they flew, Dallas opened up to him a little more. At last he felt as if he'd touched the real core of her, and not the X.O. who was his boss. "Hey, I'm a responsible kind of guy. I like long-term."

"Yeah, sure you do. How long were you married before, Cowboy?" That was his nickname in the Border Patrol.

"That's not fair."

"Sure it is. I'm a forever kind of gal. You're not, judging from your track record."

"Don't shoot me down so fast, darlin'." He saw her eyes go wide then grow warm over his endearment. Mike had discovered that Dallas needed male attention in small dollops. She didn't like brutish men, that was for sure. He never saw her go to the Nogales nightclubs to dance and drink. She stayed at the base or went to her apartment nearby, but never partied. He'd often wondered why, but now, knowing that she was incredibly responsible, dedicated to her career, and looking for a long-term relationship, he began to understand her actions.

"Hey, to me, a divorce is a sign that two people can't work out their differences. If you couldn't do it in your first marriage, Murdoch, why should I look at you as serious stuff?"

"Well," he said, eyeing her intently, "maybe you don't know the whole story behind my divorce. Maybe they don't all happen because two people are too lazy or selfish to work things out." He opened his hands. "My parents have been married since they were both eighteen, and they're fifty now. Have they had tough times? You bet. Did they struggle? Oh, yeah, I saw it. But the one thing that kept them together was that they loved one another. It's the glue that's gotten them through a lot of tough times."

"Precisely. That's what I'm talking about—commitment based on love." Dallas scanned the clearing sky. Between the gray, horizontal stratus clouds were hints of blue. In another hour they'd be out of the remnants of the hurricane and into sunshine as they made their way to Hermosillo.

She shot him a dark look. "So, if your parents are forever people, what happened to you, Murdoch?"

Okay, it was his turn to be vulnerable. Mike was uncomfortable with her flat stare, but he wanted her so damn bad, in every way, that he decided to lay the truth on the table between them. "I wanted a forever marriage, too, Dallas. I didn't plan to get married young—I figured if I married when I was older, I'd be better able to handle the rigors of it all. About five years ago, I met Galina Baranova, who was an interpreter for the Border Patrol. She was a recent immigrant from Moscow and a whiz at languages, speaking at least five fluently. I was stationed in El Paso, Texas, when I started working with her. I fell in love with her on the spot. But she wasn't who I thought she was."

"Oh?" Dallas gave him a worried glance and saw his expression go sad.

"She was with the Russian mafia." He sighed. "To make a long story short, she was an ace of a con artist. She's a genius, really. She became a mole for the Russian mafia back in Moscow. In her job as translator, she flew all over the Southwest and had access to many of the deep, dark secret records the BP kept on drug smuggling movements coming up from South America and Mexico. She was able to let her cohorts know well ahead of time when certain drug shipments were being watched, and they would change course, and we'd lose track of them. This went on for two years, until I started getting suspicious. One time, I found by accident a piece of paper in Galina's purse. I'd been digging for money in her billfold, because I was out of cash and needed some before I went to work. The paper was a list of drug smuggling operations, and she'd made a notation in one corner—the name of her contact in Mexico. We got the FBI on it, and they apprehended the dude and interrogated him back in D.C." Grimacing, Mike said quietly, "About two weeks later, the FBI came to our house and arrested Galina. They hadn't told me beforehand."

"I'm so sorry," Dallas said. She reached out and gripped his hand. "That must've been tough."

Her palm was warm and soft. Greedily, Murdoch laced his fingers with hers and gave them a gentle squeeze. This was the first time he'd ever shown his affection to Dallas. Would she realize what she meant to him? As he released her hand, he saw her blush. There was such innocence to her, despite her being a combat veteran. That was the part he wanted to access, to know, to care for, to love and cherish—forever.

The realization of how he felt slammed into him, and he tried to come to grips with it. Ever since Dallas had shown up in his life, he'd desired her. Sure, at first he had only wanted to get her to bed. But then, over the course of the last month, he had started yearning for a lot more from her. His dreams, although torrid, were about more than just sex. What he felt was much deeper than that, he realized now.

"Hey," he called softly. When Dallas turned, he saw a velvety quality in her eyes he'd never seen before. Instantly, his heart opened even wider. That mouth of hers was begging, just begging, to be kissed. Her attraction was clearly written across her suddenly very vulnerable features.

For the first time, Mike saw the real Dallas Klein. And, God forgive him, he just about died and went to heaven. "Don't feel sorry for me, darlin'. What I would like is a clean slate between the two of us. I think we cleared some important hurdles at three thousand feet here, don't you?" He flashed her an impish grin, having found out a long time ago that humor could frequently soothe a fractious confrontation. And right now, if he was reading Dallas correctly, he could see her reassessing him. Maybe even thinking about a possible relationship with him. Never had he wanted anything more.

"I'm glad we cleared the air, Mike. I didn't know the details about your divorce. That had to be horrible on you. The shock... If you entered that marriage with the idea it was forever... Well, what a heartbreaking situation."

"That's why I was hitting the Nogales nightclubs when you arrived. I was drinking to stop the pain I was feeling," he admitted quietly. After looking around, which was his habit as a copilot, he returned his gaze to her. "And you really snapped me out of it that first day we flew together." Giving her another boyish grin, he said, "Thanks. I needed that."

"What? Being laid out flat on your back on the tarmac?"

Murdoch chuckled. "Yeah, I'd been drinking heavily, almost nonstop, for two weeks. It wasn't like me, but I had to do something to dull the pain."

"Helluva way to do it," Dallas commented, searching the airspace below them. The sky was lightening up even more. The Cessna chugged like the stalwart workhorse it was. "Sometimes we all have to hit brick walls, Mike. Maybe I was your wall."

"Yeah," he murmured wryly, "but your wall has a door, and I'm knockin' to be let in, darlin'."

Chapter 4

Dallas was sitting in her office on a cold, early December morning when Mike sauntered in. She glanced at her watch and realized time was slipping away from them. As usual, he was in his rumpled flight suit, but he made it look pulverizingly male. What was there not to like about him?

"Hey, I heard some scuttlebutt from Thomas Boyce at the BP headquarters in D.C.," he said, closing the door quickly to keep in the heat. He couldn't help but stare. She was wearing a ponytail at the nape of her neck. He fantasized about removing the rubber band that held her thick, shining hair and then running his hands through it. He knew the rose-scented locks would feel like sleek, raw silk.

"Yeah? What kind of scuttlebutt?" Dallas asked, picking up her morning coffee.

Mike leaned lazily against the wooden counter where all the flight plans were created. "That you are landing us another flight team. Are we going to get in more personnel? God knows we're working 24-7, and we need the help. Our C.O. was never able to pry loose more pilots and planes from the Border Patrol because of the budget." Mike eyed her. "Is all this true?"

Grinning triumphantly, she eased back in her chair. "Sure is." She liked the way he glowed with happiness at her comment. "I've been here long enough to see that the four of us are going to be driven into the ground by the work demands." She pointed to a map behind her desk that had red pins all across the state of Sonora. "You and I have been working seven days a week since I got here."

Resting his elbows on the counter, he held her gaze. "Yeah, I can't even get a date with you because of our killer schedule," he griped good-naturedly. "That night you agreed to go to dinner with me? Our flight that day ended up lasting far past my friends' dinner hour, and it was scrubbed. When have we had time for dinner together? Much less with my friends?"

A shaft of heat moved through her. Dallas didn't tell him she was glad that long mission had happened. A part of her had been looking forward to having dinner with Mike and his Mexican friends. But another part had been reluctant. Murdoch was a macho guy who, if he saw something he wanted, went after it with no apology. While Dallas liked that kind of assertiveness in their trade, working against drug smugglers, he was moving way too fast for her on a personal front. She liked him but wasn't ready to commit to anything. Not yet. "Well," she drawled with a smile, "all in good time, Murdoch. Some things are worth waiting for. Did your parents ever try to teach you patience?" She chuckled.

"Not one of my greatest attributes, is it, Ms. Dallas?"

They were alone, and Dallas enjoyed their repartee. Mike was the biggest jokester in Nogales, and he made her laugh even at grim times chasing the druggies. "No, it's not, but you have others."

"Oh?" He perked up and placed his hands on his hips. "Like what?"

"Oh, no," Dallas said, holding up her own hands and laughing, "I'm not going there! Your head is swelled enough, Cowboy."

"I know, my arrogance is becoming. Even appealing to you. Isn't it?" Mike liked the way her cheeks grew pink. He knew how to get beneath her armor.

"At times," she said, holding his penetrating gaze and trying not to respond physically. Did Murdoch know how damn virile he was? Dallas suspected he did. Even though he'd shaved that morning, a hint of stubble already grew, making his face seem slightly dangerous. That kind of danger Dallas liked, and she quelled her yearning for him. She had to settle in as X.O., not to mention she had a number of jobs to undertake to keep this small flight unit functional.

"Well," Mike said, "since the rumor is true, where did you scrounge up these extra bodies? The C.O. has never been able to force Washington to give us relief pilots so we could have a weekend off."

"I got one pilot," she told him. "Captain Alexander. She was due for rotation out of the Black Jaguar Squadron. I knew that in advance, so I made a phone call to an influential U.S. Army general back at the Pentagon." Dallas handed him the summary orders. It was an excuse to touch his hand. The moment their fingertips met, warmth flowed into her. She savored the sensation.

"Thanks," Mike said, taking the paper. He stared down at the new orders for the pilot. "Nike Alexander?"

"It's pronounced 'Nikee.'"

"Interesting. Wasn't there a Greek goddess by that name?"

"Sure was. Nike Alexander was named after the goddess of victory. She was born in Athens. And she likes to tell everyone that the goddess was created when the god of war, Ares, consorted with a mortal woman. Nike was the child created by their love."

"She sounds like she'll be real aggressive in the air," Murdoch said, handing the sheet back to Dallas. "And if she was named after the goddess of victory, then it sounds like you picked a real winner. We want aggressive pilots around here."

"You got that right. There isn't a woman at BJS who isn't air combat aggressive, and from my experience around here, that's needed in spades. Those drug smugglers in Sonora are the worst bunch I've ever run into. And I believe Nike can help us make a difference."

"What about a copilot for her? You got one yet?"

Dallas shook her head. "No. I've got some pull in the Pentagon, and I'm working that angle right now. With the wars in Afghanistan and Iraq, pilots are rare as hen's teeth. But I've got a lead on one, and I believe we can get him."

Rubbing his hands, Mike said, "You're an accomplished, crafty woman, you know that?" He was proud of her abilities. The more he knew about Dallas, the more he admired her.

"That's the X.O.'s job," she parried, putting a number of items on her desk away. It was time to get going on their morning mission. "I like what I do. All the chess moves to get what we need around here. The C.O.'s thrilled pink we have Nike assigned to us."

"I'm sure he is. Jake and Bob are gonna be jumping up and down over this change, too. They'd like to have some time off with their families."

"I know," Dallas said, frowning. "This work is demanding. We can't be fresh and alert when we're working 24-7, either, so that's another reason to get a third flight team in here."

Giving her an intent look, Murdoch said, "You know, I got a funny feeling about you. Why do I think you aren't going to be around here forever?"

She smiled slightly as she put Nike Alexander's orders in a personnel folder, which she tucked in the file drawer on the left side of her desk. Her heart twinged at the thought of leaving Mike, and that was new for her.

Normally, Dallas considered herself a tumbleweed, moving

from one assignment to another, no strings attached. But after learning of his heartbreaking marriage, she had begun to see him in a new light. A better one. And a part of her wanted to stay here and not move when the new orders came in shortly from the Pentagon. Looking up, she said, "There's that word again—*forever*. Mike, you know in our business change is guaranteed. You might not be military, but even the ATF will switch you to another spot eventually. I'm aligned with the U.S. Army, so about every two years I'll be rotated to another base or mission."

Frowning, Murdoch took the orders for the day, which lay near his elbow, but didn't look at them. "Yet you believe in forever marriages." The idea that Dallas might leave sooner rather than later knotted his stomach. A grim feeling snaked through him, twisting his gut. For once, he wished his intuition was wrong. There was so much about Dallas that was secret or off-limits to him, even now. She had learned to trust him in the last month, and Mike couldn't fathom going up against the drug smugglers without her. She was a damn fine pilot, fierce in combat and someone he could trust to cover his back when things heated up. But it was more than that, and he tried to wrestle with the shock of her possibly walking out of his life—forever.

"Yes, but that's not a job, that's a way of life."

"I agree." Murdoch grinned. Dallas didn't seem to realize how affected he was by the thought of her leaving. But then, he'd never kissed her or really told her how he felt about her. When had there been time? Opportunity? For once, Murdoch was unhappy about the seven-day-a-week job. He wished for a day off with Dallas.

She grinned back. "Marriage should be something great to build on. That doesn't mean there won't be problems to surmount, but at least they're tackled as a team."

"On that, there's no argument." He held her gaze. "You didn't answer me. Do you know something we don't? Are you gonna pull a disappearing act on me?" That was the last thing Mike wanted, and when he saw her hesitate, his heart squeezed. She did know something.

How he wanted a relationship with this enigmatic, powerful woman. Mike knew he could be her equal. But did she?

Dallas shrugged. She knew she couldn't divulge the black ops orders that would be issued by the Pentagon. "Does it look like I'm going anywhere?" She pointed to the stack of tactical assignments on her desk. "There are all our December missions. That should tell you I'm hanging around."

"Humph." He pointed at their current mission. "Speaking of that, I see we're going back to Hermosillo."

"Yeah, our favorite place," Dallas said wryly. Getting up, she smoothed out her flight suit, picked up her helmet bag and knee board, and gave him a smile. "Ready, Cowboy?"

A prickling heat of pleasure moved through Murdoch. He liked the way she said his nickname. Throwing her a mock salute, because he was a civilian and didn't have to salute any military person, he said, "Ready, ready now…."

Murdoch was commander for the flight that day. As they snaked among the Sierra Madres looking for smugglers, Dallas scanned the terrain below. The Sonoran state, with its steep, rugged valleys, was a perfect place for low-flying drug planes to hide. They would pop up to cross a shrubby shoulder of mountain, then dive back undercover of another one. The smugglers rarely crossed into U.S. space. Instead, they'd fly to a dirt strip twenty or thirty miles south of the border and off-load their cocaine or marijuana to awaiting men, who would go by truck, horseback or foot into the USA.

Mike and Dallas had been flying for six hours by the time they neared Hermosillo. Murdoch figured they'd find something there. They always did.

"Got one," Dallas crowed, binoculars fixed on a yellow-and-white Cessna crossing a steep canyon below them. "Don't need to verify this one with authorities," she murmured, watching the plane. "The dude has the numbers on the fuselage covered over with duct tape." The Sierra Madres made an ideal place to grow marijuana, cut it, package it and then stow it on board a smuggler's plane.

"A dead giveaway he's in the trade." Tipping the wing a little, Mike spotted the plane. "Let's watch where he goes. He's heading northwest. Call *los federales*. They can get one of their twin-engine Cessnas up in the air to follow him, too." Their ATF unit frequently worked with Mexican authorities, who were learning how to hunt and capture the air smugglers, too. The U.S. had given their southern neighbor a fleet of Cessnas, twenty-six Schweizer 333 helicopters and ten refurbished Huey helicopters to aid in stopping the drug trade.

"Chances are he isn't going to one of the ninety official airports in Sonora," Dallas joked, following the smuggler's progress.

Murdoch ratcheted up the throttle to 160 miles per hour to keep up with the hedge-hopping druggie below them. "No," he drawled, "he's probably headed for one of the thousand illegal landing strips we've thus far identified." Mike smirked evilly. "Or maybe he'll show us yet another airstrip we didn't know about."

Of course, the Mexican government sent in troops to destroy the airstrips as soon as they were located. The soldiers would dig horizontal ditches across them, so planes couldn't land without crashing and tipping over on their noses.

"Nothing surprises me anymore, given their constant creativity," Dallas agreed grimly. Setting the binoculars aside, she radioed the Mexican authorities, giving a description of the smuggler's aircraft, plus latitude and longitude. After signing off, she said, "They're putting a Cessna Citation on this one."

Murdoch nodded. The U.S. had armed the Citation jet with radar.

He looked around. The day was sunny and clear, with no clouds to hamper their view. He wondered if the pilot knew they were on his six, two thousand feet above. Probably not. Often, they orbited a smuggler and let him land, and then took him on. Because they never knew where the plane would put down, it wasn't often that the *federales* could be there when they captured a smuggler.

It was dangerous work, and of late, Mike was becoming very protective of Dallas, who was just as gutsy and assertive in capturing the pilots as he was. She would blow him off if he tried to run interference for her. Still, the danger ate at him. He'd just found her; he didn't want to lose her.

"Uh-oh…" she was watching the other plane through the binoculars. "He's got a strip picked out, I think."

Frowning, Murdoch pushed the yoke forward and aimed their plane downward. "He must have spotted us. Going to land and run."

"Maybe," Dallas said. "There's a lot of sagebrush and shrubby trees in that canyon. He's got to know of a strip, but I can't see it…not yet." Her fingers tightened around the binoculars.

"I've got a bad feeling about this one," Murdoch growled. He brought the Cessna down to a thousand feet. The sides of the canyon were covered with thick brush and short green trees that could withstand the summer heat. "Where the hell is he going?"

"There it is…yeah, there's a short—very short—dirt strip at eleven o'clock on the side of the canyon. Very clever. You see it, Mike?"

Craning his neck, he squinted and finally found it. "Yeah, I do. And a couple of buildings painted desert camouflage colors next to it. This must be a major drop-off, pick-up point. A new one for us."

"I like finding the new ones," Dallas said, grinning. "Gives the Mexican Army something to do and eradicates one more loading zone for those smugglers."

Moving his hand to his left side, toward his holster, Mike muttered, "He's landing. Hang on, we're going to be on his ass shortly. Watch those buildings. There might be gunmen waiting for him. Do you see any vehicles?"

Scanning, Dallas felt the mild pull of gravity as Murdoch pushed the Cessna downward. "No…none."

"Might be hidden inside. Call *los federales* again. Let them know where we are. We may need help, but they won't get here soon enough to give it to us." Murdoch knew that it would take an hour at least to mount a troop effort into these mountains.

"Roger," she said, "we're on our own." Making a quick call, Dallas confirmed their position. By the time she got off the radio, Murdoch was bringing their Cessna in for a landing. Just ahead of them, perhaps three hundred feet away, the drug plane kicked up dust as it braked to a stop. Turning, she grabbed the two M16s. With swift efficiency, before Murdoch had even stopped their plane, she had them locked and loaded.

"Hey," he said, "be careful. Damn careful, Dallas."

She grinned. "Count on it. I'm not being taken out by a druggie."

They knew the drill and worked like a well-oiled team. Dallas opened the door and was out of it in a heartbeat, heading toward the other aircraft. Weapon raised, finger on the trigger, she ran forward, trying to keep in the pilot's blind spot until the last moment.

Murdoch was hot on her heels as they raced across the soft dirt of the recently made strip. He kept an eye on the two painted structures. Were there men inside they couldn't see? The back of his neck crawled with warning. Huffing in the higher altitude, he caught up with Dallas as they sneaked up on the tail of the other Cessna. Each wore their helmet and Kevlar flak jacket, and had plenty of weapons.

Dallas moved up one side of the fuselage, toward an emerging figure. "Halt!" she snarled in Spanish and trained her M16 on the startled copilot, who couldn't have been more than fifteen years old.

The pilot bailed when he heard Dallas's voice, pulling out a revolver as he did so. Seeing it, Murdoch leaped away from the fuselage. "Stand where you are, *hombre*," he shouted to the middle-aged man in sunglasses.

Gunfire suddenly erupted; the dirt spat up all around where Mike stood. Cursing, he leaped back against the plane. The pilot snarled a curse of his own and whirled toward him, aiming his revolver.

At once, Mike squeezed the trigger. The semiautomatic barked and jerked against his shoulder. The pilot fell, wounded.

More gunfire! Diving beneath the plane, Murdoch saw that Dallas had the youth on the ground, with plastic cuffs on his wrists. "We got company in those buildings," he shouted to her.

"I see," Dallas panted, grabbing her rifle. The only protection they had was the aircraft. Bullets flew, striking metal. The windshield shattered, sending shards of Plexiglas in all directions like shrapnel. Dallas felt some cut into her upper arm and neck.

She and Mike flattened themselves on the ground, peering from beneath the Cessna's fuselage. They trained their rifles on the buildings. Dallas gasped as she saw five men come bounding out of the doors, weapons blazing.

The smell of the rounds, the harsh bark of M16s, filled the air. The drug smugglers were running straight at them, disregarding their own safety. Dallas hugged the ground, firing short bursts and choosing her targets without letting the sudden attack rattle her. Bullets bit into the ground around her. One hit so close that dirt exploded in her face, but the dark shield of her helmet kept it out of her eyes, and she kept on shooting.

Shouts in Spanish rang out. Bullets sang like bees. Two of the smugglers fell, wounded. Three others kept charging toward them, their rifles spitting gunfire. Dallas felt everything slow down, as if she were watching a movie. And then a burning sensation flared in her left shoulder—a bullet strike. With her adrenaline pumping, it felt like the sting of an insect. She took a bead on the lead man, who was screaming angrily. He was a tall, gaunt Mexican in his early twenties, dressed in a white T-shirt, jeans and sandals. The rage in his dark brown eyes was palpable. At the same time Dallas aimed at him, he skidded to a halt, raised his rifle and aimed directly at her.

Dallas fired. And then something hit the side of her helmet. She slumped, unconscious, the rifle dropping from her hands....

Chapter 5

"Hey, Mike!" Jake called from behind the ops counter, "the Nogales hospital just called. Dallas is awake!"

Murdoch had just come in from a mission. The late afternoon sun slanted through the west window of the shack. He'd just entered the door, helmet bag in hand, and now his heart took off at a gallop. "Yeah? How is she?"

It had been two days since she'd been wounded. Two of the worst days of his life. And yet he had to fly, despite not wanting to leave her side.

Laughing, Jake put down the phone. "Awake and bitching. She wants out of there, pronto! Like yesterday. That's our X.O."

Grinning lopsidedly, Murdoch deposited his bag on the shelf. "She's okay? Talking? Her old self?"

"Sounded fine to me," Jake said, grinning widely.

"You sure?"

"Yep, no brain damage. That's good news."

"I'll get right over there. My report can wait."

Waving his hand toward the door, Jake said, "Gotcha, boss. Oh, the nurse at the desk said Dallas was asking specifically for you."

Pleasure thrummed through Murdoch. "You aren't jiving me, are you?"

"Me?" his buddy crowed. "Hell no! I swear it." He held up his fingers in the Boy Scout salute.

"You had better be telling the truth...." Murdoch growled.

Chortling, Jake said, "Take off, Mike. She wants to see you. I'll tell our C.O. what's going down and let him know Dallas is back to the land of the living. I'm sure he'll be relieved to hear that."

So was Murdoch. Lifting his hand in farewell to his friend, he exited the shack, mentally jumping up and down for joy over the good news. The day was cloudy, with rain predicted, and he found his flight suit wasn't enough to protect him from the damp chill in the air or the erratic winds. The desert could be brutally cold in winter.

Even so, Mike decided not to go back to his apartment and change into civilian clothes. He'd been on an eight-hour mission in Sonora with Bob. Since Dallas had been wounded, they were down to a three-man team once more. Nike Alexander was slated to arrive in two weeks. At least that would give them two teams in the air while Dallas was sidelined.

As Murdoch headed for his black Toyota Forerunner, his whole focus centered on Dallas. How was she? Aching to kiss her, to hold her, he felt his eyes suddenly and unexpectedly mist up with tears. He fought them back and quickly strode to his car. More than anything, he *needed* to see Dallas. To make sure she was whole and all right, despite the fact her helmet had taken a direct hit from a bullet. Would she be glad to see him?

"Mike!" Dallas called. She struggled to sit up in her bed in the private hospital room. "Am I ever glad to see you!"

Murdoch grinned unevenly as he closed the door to her small room. The sinking sun slanted through the venetian blinds to the left of her bed. Dallas was dressed in a formless blue cotton gown, with a small white square of gauze bandaged to her left temple. She was pale, but he saw the gold fire in her eyes.

"You're the most beautiful thing I've ever seen," he told her, moving to her side. Grabbing a nearby chair, he pulled it over and sat down.

Dallas smiled wanly as he bent closer and adjusted two pillows so she could lean against them. "Thanks. It's great to see you, too."

"You took a bullet to your helmet," he told her, reaching out to grasp her hand. Mike didn't care; he needed to touch her, to be reassured she was really all right. Her eyes went soft as he gripped her fingers and gave them a tender squeeze. His heart pounded briefly when she returned the gesture.

"The last thing I remember is this big dude charging me, his rifle blazing away on automatic," she murmured.

"Well," Murdoch said, "you nailed the bastard. He's dead. In fact, three of the five met their maker out there. When you went down, I finished the rest off. The *federales* got there about ten minutes later, by Huey helicopter. They cleaned up the mess." Giving her a concerned look, he added, "I didn't know if you were alive or dead, Dallas. Your helmet was cracked and blood was leaking out from beneath it. You scared me to death."

Holding his hand felt like the most wonderful thing in the world. "I'm sorry I scared you, Mike."

"You didn't do it on purpose, sweetheart." Gulping, Murdoch realized belatedly the endearment had escaped his lips. Dallas's cheeks colored briefly.

He wanted to do more than just hold her hand, dammit! Yet it had to be enough for now. And it was. His heart was soaring with happiness.

"I woke up an hour ago," Dallas confessed, holding his smoldering gaze, which made her body respond even though she was still feeling weak. "The nurse said I was calling out for you."

"Well, we *were* in the middle of a firefight," he reminded her, "and I'm sure your brain recalled that." He assumed a cocky, teasing expression. "Hey, I'm single, good-looking and available. Why wouldn't you call out for me in your moment of need?"

Dallas managed a wry smile and gripped his callused hand. She wondered what it would be like to kiss Murdoch. Suddenly smitten by the shape of his mouth, and how it moved, Dallas realized how much she liked having this guy in her life. "You're so full of yourself, dude."

"And you like me despite that, right?" He smiled wickedly. Her soft, full lips curved upward, and heat tunneled through Murdoch. Right now, Dallas was vulnerable because of her injury, and he wanted to tread lightly.

"I suppose it won't hurt to admit that I do like you a little bit," she murmured, meeting his gleaming eyes, which promised her so much. Lifting her hand, she pointed to the bandage on her temple. "Do me a favor? Get me the hell out of here. I want to go home, to my apartment. I hate hospitals, Mike. Can you talk to the physician and get me released? Please?"

Her pleading look tore at him. "Okay, I'll see what I can do. Are you in pain?"

"No. They're giving me aspirin. The nurse said I had bruised my temple. My thick skull's intact." She laughed. "For once it pays off to be hardheaded."

When Murdoch released her hand, Dallas felt as if the sun had stopped shining. He had such a positive effect on her! How could this man, who had been so difficult, suddenly mean more to her than any other guy ever had?

"Okay, boss lady, I'll go hunt down your doctor and see what I can wrangle out of him. I'll be back," he promised.

* * *

Dallas was chomping at the bit. Forty minutes had passed. What was Murdoch doing? She knew the hospital physicians were sometimes tough to track down, being so busy. Before she could work herself up anymore, the door opened and Murdoch entered. He was beaming, his mouth pulled into the broadest smile she'd ever seen.

"This looks like good news," she said, exasperation in her voice. "Is he letting me go?"

Murdoch rubbed his hands together as he came over and sat down in the chair. "Well, *she,* Dr. Maria Alvarez, is going to release you on one condition."

Dallas searched his twinkling eyes. "Okay, Murdoch, what did you finagle? There's a hitch in this. I can smell it."

He eyed her innocently. "Hey, Dr. Alvarez was pretty amicable about this idea under the circumstances. At first, when I found her, she didn't want to release you at all." He preened a little. "But with my good looks, my persuasive melt-a-woman smile, she gave in to my little plan to get you out of here."

"Uh-oh," Dallas said, swayed by that wonderful male smile herself. "Okay, what's the deal? What do I owe you?"

Murdoch chuckled. "The doctor is going to release you to me for the next twenty-four hours. She feels you need to be watched, to make sure no other symptoms manifest from that bruise to your head."

"Released to you? What does that mean?"

"I get to take you over to my apartment for the next twenty-four hours." He noted her surprise. "Don't worry, Dallas. You'll get my bedroom, and I'll sleep out on the couch. It's not what you think." Although he wished it was. Her gold eyes conveyed shock, and then her mouth set, which meant she was considering her options. "Hey," he cajoled, "it can't be that bad, can it? I'll make you chicken soup. I'm rather good at cooking, in case you didn't know. All Dr. Alvarez wants is to have a set of eyes on you to make sure you don't develop dizziness, vomiting or stuff like that. She said that normally, in a case like yours, they keep you one day for observation after you regain consciousness."

"Humph." Dallas raised an eyebrow. "Murdoch, if I didn't know better, I'd suspect you concocted this whole scheme from beginning to end."

"For once I'm innocent," Mike protested, while inwardly gloating over the situation. The beginnings of a smile curved her delicious lips. "Well? Can I sweep you off your feet, my lady? I'll carry you to my charger, and we'll blow this joint."

"Anything is better than staying here."

Giving her a hurt look, Murdoch said, "Come on. I can't be the lesser of two evils, can I?"

"That's exactly what you are," Dallas muttered.

"Then how come you look so happy?"

"Because anything's better than a hospital, that's why." Dallas grinned.

Murdoch refused to be rebuffed by her, especially since she was teasing him. He could see the joy banked in her gold eyes. "Well, I'll just have to persuade you that I'm a very good deal under the circumstances."

"Make me that chicken soup, Murdoch, and we'll talk. Okay?"

Dallas sat at the kitchen table in Murdoch's condo and savored the chicken soup. "Mmm, this is good," she murmured. "The only thing missing is my mother's matzo balls."

Mike sat at her elbow, eating a huge Caesar salad with strips of grilled chicken breast. It was nearly 7:00 p.m., but the night was young, and he was enjoying Dallas's company. "You cook much? Maybe you can teach me how to make them someday?"

"I love to cook. Just never have the time," she griped good-naturedly. When they'd gotten home, Murdoch had shown her to the bathroom, where she'd enjoyed a long, luxurious bath, washed her hair and changed into clean clothes that they'd picked up from her apartment earlier. The bandage they'd put on was waterproof, thank goodness. Dallas felt comfortable wearing a soft cotton Peruvian shift that fell to her ankles. The gold-and-purple orchids embroidered around the neckline and hem made her feel very feminine. But maybe that was due to the burning look in Murdoch's eyes. He treated her like a woman, not an air- combat commander.

Mike waved a hand toward his small and efficient kitchen. "Hey, when we start getting some time off, come on over. My mother taught me how to cook as soon as I was old enough to peer over the kitchen counter."

"Smart mom. Men should know how to cook and clean, just like any woman does."

"I keep telling you, I'm not the Neanderthal you think I am." He grinned at her lasciviously.

"I admit, I had some pretty intractable opinions about you." She finished off the soup, picked up her fork and began to help herself from his salad bowl. "I guess I'm hungrier than I thought."

"I like to share."

"Yeah, I bet you do," Dallas chuckled softly. "Hey, you make a mean Caesar dressing. You really *do* know how to cook."

"Just one more thing to love about me."

Groaning, Dallas nibbled on a piece of the savory, herbed chicken. She could taste the lemon basil. "Stop selling yourself, Murdoch. It won't do any good."

"No? What does it take to get you to fall for me, then?"

The music he'd put on was low and mellow, and she found herself relaxing even more. "Just be yourself. You don't need to convince me. I work with you every day, remember?"

"So," he said, raising his brows and spearing some romaine lettuce with his fork, "have I sold you yet?"

"You don't play fair, Murdoch." Her eyes teased him.

"No?" He sighed and enjoyed simply watching her. Dallas's hair was still damp, and it gleamed with gold highlights in the light of the chandelier. This was the first time he'd seen her in something other than a flight suit. She made that loose-fitting cotton gown look damn good. "How do I not play fair?"

"You're too blunt and forward."

"What? About liking you? About wanting to pursue something with you other than being air buddies?"

She dipped her head to hide her burgeoning smile. "You just don't take no for an answer, do you?"

"Never. Not when it's something I want."

"You're a wild man, Murdoch. The C.O. named you and your friends well—the Wild Bunch."

"But you love wild, Dallas. From what you've told me about the Black Jaguar Squadron, it's a bunch of wild *women*. You go for primal." He met her laughter-filled eyes. How badly he wanted to get up, lift her out of that chair and kiss her silly.

"Point taken. We are wild women. The whole premise of the BJS was cooked up by Major Maya Stevenson, and she's as wild as they come."

"Yes," Murdoch said patiently, "and you were her X.O. for six years, so what does that make you?"

Dallas held up her hand. "Okay, guilty as charged."

"So, why wouldn't a wild man and a wild woman find happiness in a relationship with one another?" he posed archly, pointing his fork in her direction. Dallas was hungry and eagerly consuming a good portion of his salad, but Mike didn't mind. She was alive. She was getting well. That was all that mattered to him.

"I suppose they might," she admitted. She wasn't tasting the delicious salad anymore, her heart and body were reacting to Murdoch's nearness. It seemed as if she were sitting next to sunlight; she felt warm, soft and achy in all the right places. And he damn well knew that she was enamored with him.

The only thing that held Dallas back was that shortly, the Pentagon was going to assign her somewhere in the world with a new Black Jaguar Squadron. What then? Mike loved his job. He was a civilian. He had a life here in Arizona, where he'd been born and raised. She figured he wouldn't want to pull up his roots and become an aimless tumbleweed, following her around the globe. Past experience had shown her that few men would ever consider such a scenario.

Frustration thrummed through Murdoch. How to convince this feisty, no-nonsense woman to fall into his arms and allow him to love her until she melted like hot wax? "I have an idea. A proposition of sorts."

Dallas sat back and drank from her iced tea glass. Seeing the playful look of hurt on his handsome face, she said, "What idea?"

"Christmas is coming up shortly. I make a mean turkey stuffed with cranberries, apples and raisins. How about you agree to come over for a great gourmet dinner midafternoon Christmas Day, and consider staying overnight afterward?"

Chapter 6

"Merry Christmas, Dallas!" Nike Alexander called as she entered the ops shack. "BJS rides again, only in disguise here in Nogales. How are you?" She grinned widely at her old X.O., who had been working behind the ops desk.

"Nike!" Dallas jumped up and quickly rounded the desk, throwing her arms about the Greek woman. "Hey, you're two days early!" She stepped back and beamed at the black-haired, brown-eyed helicopter pilot. Cut short with a few wispy bangs across her broad forehead, Nike's hair shone like a raven's wing.

"Yeah, I couldn't stand all that time off," she griped good-naturedly, tossing her helmet bag on the desk. "I'm a trauma junkie. All BJScrs are. We live to fight. Fight to survive. You know that. I just came off a thirty-day leave ten days early. I loved going home to Athens. My parents and big brothers and their wives threw me all kinds of parties—drinking, dancing, feasting…. They all wanted me to stay through Christmas. But I started to pine away for some ass-kicking action." She laughed and gripped Dallas's upper arm. "It's so good to see you again! I really didn't want to leave BJS, you know?"

"No one does," Dallas said, smiling at the pilot. "Coffee?" She had decorated the ops office for the holidays, draping silver tinsel across the two windows, hanging plastic mistletoe above the counter. She made sure some upbeat Christmas music played on their CD player. The crews really appreciated a woman's touch.

"Well, it isn't Greek coffee, but I'm hoping since you're X.O. here you at least got good South American espresso?" She peered hopefully toward the coffee station behind the ops desk.

Chuckling, Dallas poured them some of the freshly made brew. "Oh, you can count on that, Nike." She handed her a cup. "Great Brazilian coffee, no less."

"Thanks. Hey, I just met Bob and Jake over in the hangar. They're getting ready for this morning's mission." She squinted. "What's this about you getting wounded? You look fine to me."

Sipping her coffee, Dallas sat down at her desk. "It was nothing. Just a graze from a druggie's bullet. He and I were firing at each other at pretty much point-blank range." She touched her temple. "This happened two weeks ago. It's all healed up and I'm fine, so no worries."

"Whew!" Nike said. She leaned against the counter, holding the cup between her small, delicate-looking hands. "So, I heard some scuttlebutt down at BJS just before I left. Is it true? Are the boys at the Pentagon giving serious consideration to the formation of a second BJS unit? And are you slated to be its C.O.? Please, please, tell me it's true because…" she looked around the cramped office and lowered her voice "…as much as I appreciate coming here and flying a fixed wing, I'd much rather have an Apache helo strapped to my butt, doing real combat."

"Yes, it's true, but keep that top secret between you and me." Raising her finely shaped black brows, Nike flashed a wide smile. "You know us BJS women—we live together, we die together. We're tight. No worries. So, am I on your short list to go with you?"

"You're on the list," Dallas murmured with a smile. "Again, top secret info at this point."

"Gotcha. Hey, your friend Major Kat Wallace is doing special duty right now over in Virsland. Sounds like there's some hot action going on over there." Nike rubbed her hands together. "You think the Pentagon will put the second BJS squadron in Europe somewhere? I'm itching to put my hand back on a Gatling gun and missiles, to fire at the baddies. I'm so addicted to stress."

Holding up her palm, Dallas said, "I just got a call from someone in the Pentagon who's in on the planning. He told me yesterday that it's looking good to have BJS in Europe or Afghanistan for the first of next year. That's all he told me."

"I sure hope it's in the Baltic region."

Dallas grinned sourly over her officer's enthusiasm; Apache pilots were known for their fierce, assertive attitudes. "My unnamed source told me that some of the women who are graduating soon from Apache school are slated to be assigned to me and the new BJS unit. They are military pilots from various countries, just like our first BJS unit was. A little United Nations of sorts, which makes me happy."

"How cool!" Nike did a little dance, waving her arms above her head. Coming back to the desk, she grew more serious. "Okay, so between now and the first of the year, we play in Mexico's backyard, chasing the baddies in our putt-putt Cessnas, right?"

"Something like that." Dallas smiled. "Your new partner, Captain Charlie Steinway, has already arrived. I'm pairing you up with him. He's the father of two cute girls, and his wife is an accountant who just got a job in a Nogales legal firm. I think you'll like him. He's easygoing."

"Don't tell me he's a throwback Neanderthal."

"Nope, he's a progressive male, Nike. He won't be prejudiced against you or your experience. Charlie is open to women doing it all."

"My kind of guy." And then she blew air out between her lips. "Speaking of guys. Damned if I can find a good one to have a long-term relationship with, Dallas. You know those Latino men down in Peru are to die for, but they aren't about to leave their huge extended families and become globetrotters with the woman they profess to love."

"Don't I know that one." Dallas remembered all the pain over her old lover and his angst about leaving his family to follow her on her career path outside Peru.

"Those Latin studs were great for dancing and partying, but forget the rest," Nike griped. "I'm twenty-eight. I keep having dreams about finding a dude who loves me as I am and will follow me to the ends of the earth, no questions asked."

"Oh," Dallas said with a laugh, "that is the problem. Men haven't come that far yet, from what I can see." She thought about Murdoch. Her heart wanted him. Her body wanted him. She even dreamed about making love with him. Would Mike follow her to her next assignment, somewhere in Europe or wherever the Pentagon eventually placed the new BJS squadron? Dallas wasn't sure he would, which was why she was putting the brakes on their relationship.

Christmas was only two days away. Her heart sped up in anticipation. No question, she wanted to go to bed with Murdoch.

In a few short months, he had turned from caveman and frog into a handsome prince before her very eyes. He was everything she'd ever wanted in a man. But the great question was did he love her? Enough to leave his job with the Border Patrol and follow her to her next military assignment? That, she wasn't at all sure of.

"Are you flying on Christmas Day?" Nike asked.

"Not planning on it. As X.O., I make out the mission plans, and I persuaded the C.O. to give everyone the day off. We've been at this 24-7, Nike. Everyone is tired."

"Getting replacements will help ease that situation, though," her friend pointed out, sipping her coffee with relish.

"Right on. I still want to give the guys time off for the major holidays if I can."

"You know Navarro, though," Nike warned, setting her white mug down on the counter. "He knows the *norte americano* penchant for being softies on big holidays. That's when he usually mounts a huge air campaign to get drugs out of a country or move them from one place to another. You do recall that?"

"Yes, I do," Dallas said, worriedly looking through some of her paperwork. "If I get a call from the *federales* that their radar is picking up a lot of Cessnas in the air on Christmas Day, well, I'm going to have to change gears and ask everyone to come in and fly. I don't want to, though."

"Navarro doesn't know you're up here at the other end of the line, making chess moves on him, I'll bet."

"He may or may not. But druggies have eyes and ears everywhere. If he knows I'm here, he'll expect we'll interdict him on holidays. I'm hoping Navarro will remember past experience in Peru and stay on the ground all through Christmas."

"It's a feint strategy," Nike said, nodding her head. "A good one."

Holding up her crossed fingers, Dallas said, "Definitely. But if Navarro doesn't know I'm at the helm up here on the border, he's going to throw every Cessna he owns into the air on the twenty-fifth."

"Well, we'll find out, won't we?" Nike said, finishing off her coffee.

"This sucks," Murdoch muttered. He was commander that day, and a cold front in the area was making the air bumpy. They were flying over the Sierra Madres, where rain and snow had been forecasted for the entire region. It was a lousy day, with gray, low-hanging clouds wreathing the mountaintops, fog blanketing canyons and valleys below. The Cessna bucked even in his skilled hands. "I make a fabulous Christmas dinner with the best stuffing in the world, and you call us all back to work." He slanted a humorous glance toward Dallas who was scanning the terrain through the binoculars. "What are you? A sadist?" he teased.

Sighing, Dallas lowered the field glasses and glanced over at him. She couldn't get enough of being in Murdoch's presence, and yet when he was this close, her pulse went crazy. Her body ached with need, and her heart skittered with each heated look they exchanged. "Navarro launched ten Cessnas from the Hermosillo area. What was I to do when the *federales* called me at 0500 this morning? Navarro thinks we're grounded and eating turkey or ham today. That's why he launched this major move."

"Yeah," Mike said, "I know, I know. It's not your fault, Dallas. It's just that I spent hours over the last couple of days preparing our meal. The wine's chilled. Everything's ready to pop in the oven...." He had visions of taking Dallas to bed as dessert. For her and him. Now, it was blown all to hell. Murdoch wanted to wrap his hands around Navarro's neck and throttle the son of a bitch for ruining his romantic plans. He couldn't figure out why Dallas was so hesitant. He saw desire in her eyes. Why wasn't she giving him the signal to come and get her?

Dallas squeezed Mike's forearm, the muscles of which leaped and hardened beneath her touch. How she wanted to explore the rest of him. Murdoch was in top shape. Since he'd stopped drinking, he ran five miles every morning, long before the sun rose. The Nogales office had a weight lifting room and he used it religiously. "There will come a time when we'll be able to stand down. Just have patience."

Curling his lip in a sneer, Murdoch swiveled around to see if he could spot drug planes hip-hopping through the rugged canyons and valleys. Rain began to splatter the cockpit windshield. He was hoping if the visual dropped below allowable conditions dictated in the Instrument Flight Rules, they'd get to go home, and maybe his Christmas plans wouldn't be ruined, after all. Right now, despite the increasing rain, they had a good three miles of visibility, and that wouldn't send them home early. "Patience, my ass. I feel like a hungry vulture with a meal sitting down below, but I can't get at it."

Laughing, Dallas went back to hunting for smugglers with her binoculars. "You're incorrigible, Murdoch." She felt the Cessna bucking from the strong winds. At higher altitudes, the mountains were swathed in thick blankets of snow.

"Yeah, but I know you love me anyway."

Dallas prickled beneath his teasing. "Love? First time you've used that word with me, Murdoch. You aren't just throwing it around, are you? Men sometimes do that. They say, 'Oh, I love you,' just to get a woman to bed."

Banking the aircraft to the left, Murdoch slid a thousand feet lower. The mighty Sierra Madres bracketed them as they moved into a long, narrow canyon. The winds increased and the aircraft became harder to handle. It would shoot upward fifty feet when it hit an air pocket, and he'd have to stabilize it. "I don't use that word like it was popcorn at a movie, Ms. Dallas."

Dallas chuckled. "Okay…"

"Love is a commitment."

"It certainly is."

"What does love mean to you?" Murdoch asked her curiously. He noted how her lips tensed as she peered through the binoculars.

"Love means a forever thing to me, Murdoch, through good and bad times. It means you follow your loved one no matter where they go in the world."

"That's an interesting definition."

"My mother followed my father when he worked as a spy in a number of European countries. She did so because she loved him."

"I see." Frowning, Mike rubbed his nose and then placed his hand back on the yoke. "And did he ever follow her on an assignment? You said they're still in the Mossad."

"Yep, my father followed my mother when she was assigned to the Baltic region of Europe. Their love was such that they didn't care where they were in the world so long as they were together."

"That's important to you?" he asked soberly, expecting an honest answer from her.

Her smile disappeared. "It's everything."

"Well," Murdoch said blithely, "you're here and so am I. I'm not going anywhere and neither are you. So it's a perfect situation to think about a relationship. Don't you agree?"

Inwardly, Dallas grimaced at his lightly spoken words. She was under orders from the Pentagon to say nothing of the top secret move to place a second BJS squadron somewhere in the world. "Yes, it's perfect," she said without enthusiasm.

Murdoch's intuition niggled at him. Though he wanted to pursue the topic, he got back to the business of flying. With the changing wind conditions, the ragged spires of the rocky canyon they were flying through could rip a plane apart if a pilot wasn't paying attention. The rain increased and visibility lessened, perhaps to a mile now. And if that wasn't all, the weather, which had been ugly to begin with, turned threatening. Raindrops continued to splatter across the Plexiglas windshield. Secretly, he hoped they would turn to ice crystals. If they did, he and Dallas would have to fly lower to stop ice from gathering on their wings, and head straight home. The Cessna did not have heaters in the wings, and that meant the danger of crashing if ice began to build up on them.

Mentally, Murdoch crossed his fingers. Black clouds from the west were rolling toward them in a large, churning bank. Maybe the temperature would drop even more. He noted the outside temperature was hanging at forty-five degrees Fahrenheit.

"What a rotten day," he growled unhappily. "Instead of being in my nice, warm apartment, with the turkey roasting in the oven, sending that wonderful smell throughout the place, we're here in some of the nastiest smuggling country in Mexico. We could be hanging the decorations right now on the tree I just bought. Christmas music would be playing in the background. I'd ply you with a great wine. We'd kiss under the mistletoe and then enjoy a tasty dinner. Afterward, well…"

"You're such a dreamer, Murdoch." Dallas gave him a tender look. She saw his eyes smolder with intensity. There was no question he wanted her—in every way. And didn't she want him, too? Oh, yes. Far too much for her own good. But her future was about to change, and she wasn't at all convinced Murdoch and their fragile new relationship would survive it.

"You know, you're always in my dreams," he confided to her in a serious tone. Her gold eyes widened and then grew soft. Aching to kiss her, he reached out and skimmed her strong jaw with his fingers. "You *are* my dream come true, Dallas. You have to know that by now."

Pleasant tingles radiated from where he'd stroked her. Unconsciously, Dallas touched the area and then settled the binoculars in her lap. "Maybe we need to talk, Mike. Serious talk. Not teasing like usual, okay?"

Shrugging, he said, "I'm all ears, Dallas. What do you want to talk about? Us, I hope?"

Dallas was about to speak when suddenly, the engine sputtered nastily. Tensing, she saw smoke leaking from beneath the cowling.

"Damn," Murdoch snarled, quickly moving into emergency landing procedures. "Call base. Tell them we've got serious engine problems…."

Chapter 7

Murdoch quickly feathered the engine. Thick black smoke roiled from beneath the cowling, making it hard to see. Cursing, he vaguely heard Dallas call the Nogales base and give them critical information. As he glanced down, he saw a possible place to land at the end of the canyon.

Heart thundering, he wrestled the Cessna down to six hundred feet. The massive, rugged yellow-and-ochre walls of the canyon rose around them now, and the winds were erratic. Sweat popped out on his upper lip. There was no sound, just the hammering of the rain against the aircraft. The prop whirled lazily in the wind, as they free-floated on the air currents. The altimeter was rapidly unwinding. They were now at five hundred feet, on a gentle glide downward.

"Tighten your harness," he growled.

"Done," Dallas said, tight-lipped. She saw a small patch of flat land at the end of the canyon. "You heading for that box area?"

"Got it," he said, hands tight on the yoke. Attempting a dry stick landing, one without an engine, was dangerous under any circumstances, but here… The rain increased. Four hundred feet.

"Damn, talk about low vis," he growled.

"Bad," she agreed. Gripping the arm of her seat, Dallas could do nothing but watch. Murdoch was the pilot, and it was his responsibility to get them down safely. But could he? The wind slammed against them.

"Dammit," he muttered. Three hundred feet.

The Cessna slid to the right, the wing tip suddenly dipping.

Instantly, he played with the rudders. The craft righted. Two hundred feet.

He was off course! The wind had blown him from the center trajectory he'd put the plane in. Instantly, he banked to the left, played again with the rudders. They skimmed a hundred feet above the rocky desert floor.

Dallas saw the box canyon approaching. It was dotted with cactus and brush, and some chunks of rock that could tear the landing gear from beneath the Cessna. She tensed, gripping the seat and bracing.

"Hang on!" Murdoch rasped. Fifty feet.

If only the wind wouldn't nail them! He wrestled with the controls as the ground suddenly came up at them. The stall buzzer started screeching because he'd brought the Cessna in nose high. At all costs, he didn't want the tricycle landing gear torn off or they'd go nose-diving into the unforgiving desert floor. The screeching continued. The Cessna lugged, and forward motion slowed remarkably. Twenty feet.

At the last moment, he dropped the nose of the plane. The warning shriek ceased.

Silence reigned, except for the battering rain.

And then…

They were down! The landing gear settled in. Murdoch was

so tense it felt as if he would snap in two. He played the yoke and rode the rudders as if stepping on fragile eggs. The Cessna raced along the rocky, rough ground.

"Look out!" Dallas yelled, pointing ahead. A hundred feet in front of them a large rock lied. Large enough to do them major damage.

Too late! Murdoch hadn't seen the rock because of the low visibility. As he slammed his feet on the rudders, the nose whipped downward. The propeller dug into the earth and shattered, sending metal flying in all directions.

The landing gear grated and snapped off.

Suddenly, the aircraft skewed to the right, the wing tip digging into the muddy gravel. Cursing, Murdoch hung on, no longer able to control the Cessna.

A grating roar, the sound of rock ripping the lightweight aluminum belly of the aircraft, filled the cabin. Murdoch felt the wing snap off; the metallic screech hurting his ears. More than anything, he didn't want Dallas hurt.

The harness bit savagely into his shoulders and across his waist as the aircraft hit the wall of the box canyon then shuddered in its death throes. It finally settled with scraping, shrill sounds against the rocks, then quiet prevailed.

Dallas shook her head, trying to get her bearings. The fuselage cowling was bent up and ripped open. Her side of the Cessna was smashed against the canyon wall. The door was impossible to open, the window shattered and rain pouring in.

"You okay?" Murdoch asked, unsnapping his harness and scanning her quickly. She looked pale but composed.

"Fine, just a few bruises. You?"

"Okay. Let's egress," he ordered.

"Roger that."

Murdoch used his shoulder to pop the pilot's door open. No more smoke was coming from the engine, which was good, but they couldn't risk staying put. The possibility of explosion was high; he could smell aviation fuel inside and outside the cabin. Turning, he gripped Dallas's extended hand, and she leaped out beside him.

"Let's get the survival gear from the rear compartment," he told her. Rain was wetting his hair and clothing. The temperature was chilly, and the drenching only made him colder. Dallas beat him to the compartment. She twisted the handle, and the door fell open.

Reaching inside, Murdoch hefted the large, dark green waterproof bag over his shoulder. He started to search for a safe, dry place to shelter.

"Over there," Dallas said, running ahead of him.

There was a cave on the other side of the canyon, about two hundred feet away. Far enough from the plane that, in case it did explode, they would be safe from any debris or shrapnel. Trotting through the muck and puddles, and dodging jagged rocks, Murdoch closed the distance between them.

"Phew!" Dallas said, happy to reach the dry cave. She turned and waved as Murdoch came in out of the rain. He dropped the rubberized bag on the ground between them and sank down beside it. "Merry Christmas, Happy Hanukkah," she said, grinning as she knelt opposite him.

"I'm celebrating," Mike told her, giving her a tense, twisted smile. He removed his helmet and set it aside, then started digging items out of the bag. "We're alive. We walked away from this crash. Always a good time to celebrate."

"Ditto. But no turkey dinner tonight, Murdoch."

The adrenaline made him shaky in the aftermath. He noticed Dallas's hands were trembling, too. "Don't even go there," he jested. "Damn, I wish they'd put a bottle of good, mellow whiskey into this survival kit," he muttered. "I could use a stiff shot right about now to settle my nerves. How about you?"

"Roger that," she said, breathless. "I'm starting to have adrenaline letdown." She shook her hands rapidly for a moment. "Realizing we survived, Mike. I was scared."

"Me, too." He flashed her a tender look. Dallas's color was coming back. She removed her helmet and set it nearby. The flak jacket came off next. "Did I ever tell you that you sure as hell make a shapeless flight suit look great?" he growled.

Chuckling, Dallas felt heat roll into her face. She saw the glint of a hunter was in Murdoch's eyes. "Thank you—I think."

Sitting back on his heels, he glanced out the mouth of the cave. "Look! Snow! Merry Christmas, Happy Hanukkah, to you! I might not have a turkey dinner and wine for you, but hey, this isn't bad." He gestured toward the huge snowflakes twisting and dancing in the gusts of wind.

"Snow…!" She wrinkled her nose and grinned at him. The rain made the planes of his face gleam. Murdoch looked dangerously attractive.

"Hey, just consider me your Christmas present." He opened his arms wide.

Her laughter echoed through the cave. "You're incorrigible even under these circumstances." She shook her head and started checking on their supplies; there were enough for a week at least.

"Aren't you inspired?"

Dallas snorted. "Not unless you can produce a red ribbon to put in your hair, Cowboy."

Murdoch's mouth curved faintly. "We can imagine, can't we?"

It felt good to Dallas to indulge in their usual banter. They'd survived a crash! "We'll see," she murmured. Reaching for a GPS radio in the mix of items, she held it up. "I got a message off to Nogales before we went down. They know where we are."

"They can't mount a rescue right now," Murdoch said, eyeing the weather outside the cavern. "None of the *federale* helos have IFR instrumentation. Our base will probably contact them, and they'll get here tomorrow morning, after it stops snowing."

Nodding, Dallas pulled out the silver blankets that kept in body heat. "You're right. So we're spending Christmas in a cave."

"At least we're alive, unhurt and together." He sighed, admiring the graceful way her hands moved. "Not a bad combo."

"Right," Dallas said. "You want to start a fire? My blood has thinned from six years of living in the jungle, and I can't take the cold like I used to."

Murdoch got to his feet. "I can't have my woman cold."

The cave had been used by wild animals over the years; he could see dried scat here and there. The cavern wound back a good fifty feet, becoming smaller and smaller as he ambled toward the rear wall. Lucky for them, plenty of dry sticks and branches lay about. As he brought back the fuel, he noticed Dallas had already found dried brush just inside the cave entrance.

Mike began to see this unexpected situation as a great opportunity. First off, a fire and getting dry. Then something to eat….

As he started working on the fire, he hummed Christmas tunes to himself.

"Well, Christmas dinner hasn't been all that bad," Dallas said. The firelight was throwing deep shadows across the cave. She sat next to Murdoch on a log he'd dragged up to the fire. Outside, it was dark, and the snow was letting up.

Murdoch pushed the beans around on his makeshift plate. "MREs are never good," he muttered. "I keep thinking about that herb-rubbed turkey, my excellent dressing I spent a day on, all going to waste."

After finishing off her meal of spaghetti, Dallas took a sip of her coffee from her aluminum cup. "There's always another day, Mike. You're giving your gourmet meal its last rites?"

Chuckling, he said, "Does that mean you'd come over for a post-Christmas gourmet dinner at my place once we get home?"

"Sure. Why not?"

"Wow. This is new. What happened?" He reached up and tapped her brow, touching her dark hair in the process. "Are you sure you didn't hit the windshield and bump your noggin?"

Dallas caught his hand and squeezed it. "No, Cowboy, I didn't. I'm not out of my mind, as you're implying."

Holding her hand on her thigh, Mike said, "Maybe this little crash woke you up, then?"

"Maybe," she agreed. She liked the way his strong, warm fingers felt wrapped around her own. Their flight suits had dried out hours ago, thanks to a good fire. The temperature was rising now that the cold front had passed through.

Murdoch set down his plate. "I'm entertaining a thought, Dallas."

"Uh-oh, here we go…."

"Ah, come on. Indulge me and my fantasies."

Giggling, she said, "Okay, what's your idea?"

He took her hand and rested it on his thigh. "We have two foil space blankets. How about we spread one on the cave floor and huddle beneath the second one? We can stay warmer by sharing our body heat."

She met his dark gaze and grinned. "That's funny, I was thinking the same thing, Cowboy. How about that?"

"You're such a tease, Klein."

"Me?" She feigned shock.

"You're as bad as I am, and you know it."

She liked the way his mouth drew into a boyish smile. The gleam in his blue eyes sparked a hot response. "I like the idea."

"Good, so do I."

If nothing else, the crash had ripped away Dallas's fear of having a relationship with Mike. Life was too short. One or both of them could be badly injured or even dead right now. And they weren't. "I don't know where all this will lead," she confided to him, dropping her teasing tone. Dallas searched his eyes.

He squeezed her hand reassuringly. "I don't either, Dallas. But you know what? I'm open to a future with you. Being around you is like living with a lightning bolt. I never know what will happen next." His voice lowered. "What I can't live with is the thought of not having you in my life."

"Even if I am the proverbial lightning bolt?"

He lifted her hand and kissed the back of it gently. "Some people are catalysts, darlin', and you're one of them." His voice deepened to a growl. "What is important to me is you, Dallas. That's the bottom line."

Her heart opened and a soft sigh issued from her lips. "Do you always say the right thing at the right time?"

"No. Look at how we crashed into one another on that first day." Murdoch flashed her a wicked grin.

"Point taken," she admitted, returning his smile. "But you changed."

"Yes, because you were right, and I was wrong. You're a fair-minded person. You forgive past mistakes, and you don't throw salt in a person's wounds. You forgive, forget and move on. I've never met a woman like that. And not that many men, now that I think about it."

"It's not productive, hanging on to the past," Dallas murmured. Her hand was tingling wildly where he'd pressed that lingering caress. What would it be like to kiss those male lips of his?

"How about we take this a day at a time?" Mike suggested.

"Roger that."

"Good. You want to make that satellite call to Nogales?" They had checked in by GPS earlier with the C.O. and had promised one last nighttime transmission to let him know they were safe.

"Yes, I'll do it this time." She reluctantly released Mike's hand.

"You take care of business, and I'll take care of our bed."

Dallas saw the little-boy smile on his mouth grow. "Sounds perfect, Mike. Go for it." She went to the pack for the GPS phone. Stepping to the cave entrance, to pick up transmission, Dallas made the call.

Murdoch had put the finishing touches on their bed when she turned and walked back to him. She was smiling broadly.

"Good news. *Los federales* say they'll be here around 1100 tomorrow morning to pick us up, by helo. They'll take us to Hermosillo, where Nike and Charlie will meet us and fly us back to Nogales." She switched off the GPS and tucked it into the pack.

"We'll consider this our roughing-it-in-the-wild experience," he suggested, watching her come toward him. Her flight suit had a zipper and his fingers literally itched to start pulling it downward.

Dallas's entire body tingled beneath Murdoch's dark, animal-istic look. In the privacy of a remote canyon, with no one to inter-rupt them, she could finally consummate with Mike Murdoch all she felt for him. His delicious mouth curved upward at the corners as she slipped her arms around his broad shoulders.

"Now," she whispered, taking full advantage of her height and pressing herself wantonly against his male form. "Right now…" His mouth swept down on hers like a hawk upon its prey. Except she was no victim, nor was he her enemy. Predator, yes, but so was she. A soft moan rose in her throat as his mouth moved com-mandingly against her own. Matching his strength, relishing the warmth of his lips, Dallas felt his hands, long and lean, curve around her rib cage.

The scent of him, the taste of coffee, the dryness of the cave and the freshness of the rain-washed air combined in a mix of pleasurable sensations. As his tongue swept across her lower lip, she smiled, and his eyes shone with fierce blue fire. Together the two of them sank to the blanket, facing one another. He tore his mouth from hers and pulled the other silver blanket over them.

Mike had thoughtfully rolled up their nylon jackets into makeshift pillows. As he settled back down, his arm beneath her neck, he reached for the zipper at her throat.

"You have no idea how long I've dreamed about doing this," he told her huskily, and then captured her mouth with his once more.

Dallas's skin burned with need as he slowly, agonizingly slowly, pulled the zipper tab downward. He brushed the skin between her breasts. Threading her fingers through his dark, mussed hair, she inhaled his masculine scent, her nostrils flaring as she drank him in thirstily. When his hand reached her abdomen, Dallas moaned again.

Without hesitation, Murdoch slid his large, rough palm inside her flight suit, exploring her flesh. His fingers wreaked pleasure everywhere he touched. When he finally grasped her hip and drew her tightly against him she felt the hardness of his arousal and responded instantly. His lips curved, and she smiled with him.

"Now," Dallas whispered against his mouth, "it's my turn." She found the zipper of his own flight suit and just as slowly opened it. Bit by bit she drew the tab down, the material apart, to explore his hairy chest. His muscles leaped beneath her caresses.

By the time she'd gotten the zipper down to his crotch, he was groaning. Barely able to think herself, Dallas felt him slide his hand beneath the shoulder of her flight suit and ease it off. She mimicked his actions. In no time, they had kicked the garments off their feet and pushed them aside. Dallas never wore lingerie beneath her flight suit. She hated such constraints.

"Dreams do come true," Murdoch murmured, kissing her cheek, her delicate earlobe, and then trailing a series of nips down her slender neck. He delighted in the erratic pulse beneath her smooth, soft skin. Though his own body was hard and aching, he wanted to slow himself down to please her thoroughly. This was about what he held in his heart for this courageous woman warrior.

She was so incredibly soft in all the right places…. His hand moved to cup one of her luscious, taut breasts, and she sighed in response. Murdoch wouldn't disappoint her. No, he wanted to continue to hear her moan, hear her gasps of delight and feel her fingers digging convulsively into his tense shoulders.

As he moved Dallas onto her back, Murdoch looked down into her slitted, golden eyes, framed by those thick lashes. His gaze lingered on her parted lips, which gleamed from his kisses. Satisfaction soared through him as she slid her arms around his shoulders and pulled him down to her. She was unafraid to meet him as an equal.

His whole body radiating tension, Murdoch groaned as he thrust deeply into her. A cry escaped her lips and she wrapped him in her arms, keeping him close as they moved together rhythmically. Before Mike knew it, a wild, heated vibration had begun in his lower body, changing to tremors and then a powerful earthquake. As he felt her tense with pleasure, his release began, an explosion of heat. Eyes closed, he felt every cell of her soft, liquid core surrounding him. The sensations were like powerful waves hitting the beach, one after another, rolling through him. The heat was scalding, and he growled with pleasure....

Gradually, Murdoch became aware he was lying on Dallas, and he rolled off, drawing her into his arms. He wrapped the silver blanket around her exposed shoulders.

Firelight danced and leaped against the cave walls. Though her face was shadowed, her eyes burned with fierce desire. Dallas threaded her fingers through his damp hair, and then pressed her palm to his cheek.

"You are something else, Cowboy," she whispered, sliding her lips across his. Her entire body felt like effervescent champagne. Dallas absorbed the sensation of his hard male planes against her softer, rounded ones as they snuggled together beneath the blanket. She rested her cheek against his shoulder and gazed up into his smoldering blue eyes. There was such warmth radiating from him that she didn't feel the cold of the cave. Brushing her hand across his perspiring face, his rugged jaw, she whispered, "What a wonderful gift. Thank you…."

Murdoch smoothed her mussed hair away from her face. He saw the satisfaction in her eyes and heard it in her husky voice. "We're a gift to one another, darlin'."

With a sigh, Dallas relaxed in his arms. The firelight created shadowy flickers against the rock walls of the cave. The snapping and popping of the wood was pleasant and soothing. "It's nice to be able to fall asleep in your arms," Dallas whispered, closing her eyes.

Murdoch cuddled her close, curving his arm over her back and shoulder. For a long time, he lay there, just listening to her breathe. Her hair tickled his chin, and each moist, warm exhalation caressed his flesh. All these things he'd imagined before this, yet the real thing surpassed them all. Mike felt like the richest man in the world. It was one helluva Christmas and Hanukkah, after all.

Chapter 8

"So, when were you going to tell me you'll be leaving?" Mike asked. Outside the cave, the dawn sky was gray. The worst weather had passed as they slept in one another's arms. It had been the best night of his life.

Dallas had just climbed back into her flight suit, and so had he. She stared at him across the fire, which he was bringing to life with some twigs. Her heart thudded in response to the serious look in his eyes. Pulling the zipper up to her throat, she sat down on the twisted silver blankets, where they'd made love twice. She took one olive-green sock and pulled it onto her right foot.

"I was trying to think of a way to broach the subject," she admitted quietly.

Mike continued to add bits of twigs, which flamed to life on the coals. "I finally found out why you'd been so standoffish for so long."

"It was top secret. How did you find out?" She put on the other sock and watched a slight smile crawl across that wonderful mouth of his.

"I can't tell. I have my sources, though. Don't forget I was an Apache helo pilot myself before I left the U.S. Army and joined the Border Patrol. Ten years in the military teaches you a lot." He snapped a couple more twigs and dropped them on the growing flames. "I still have friends in the Pentagon."

"I see. They must be heavyweights, then."

"You could say that."

"You're enjoying this too much, Murdoch."

"Am I?" He rose lithely and went to the stash of larger limbs he'd gathered the night before.

Dallas sat there, legs drawn up, arms resting across her knees. She watched him walk back to the fire. Outside, the day was dreary but not rainy. At 0700 it was cool but not freezing. "Yes, you are."

"I'm sorry, darlin'. I shouldn't be teasing you like this."

"Especially before I've got coffee percolating through my veins."

His mouth curved briefly. "You're going to get orders on January 2 to head up Black Jaguar Squadron 60." He looked up and held her narrowed eyes. "They've given you a number designation. Did you know that?"

"No." Frowning, she studied Murdoch in the gathering silence. Only the wood popping, snapping fire broke it. "Okay, wise guy, how come you know so much?"

He gloated. "Major Dane York is a friend of mine. Has been ever since we flew Apaches together back at flight school."

"Oh." Dallas quickly put the rest together. Dane York had married Maya Stevenson, commanding officer of the Black Jaguar Squadron in Peru. "It appears you and Dane talk often."

Mike shrugged. "We do keep in touch. He called me a week ago to let me know that Maya was promoted to lieutenant-colonel, and both of them are leaving Peru and heading to the

Pentagon for a two-year assignment." Murdoch held her gaze. "Maya and Dane will be your ops and planning contacts when BJS 60 goes live."

Surprised at the information, Dallas digested it a long time before speaking. "Where are they putting the new squadron?"

"Afghanistan. At a secret base near Mazar-e-Sharif. It will be a jump-off point for you and your women to get to Turkmenistan, Uzbekistan or Tajikistan in a hurry. That's the next area the Pentagon thinks terrorists are going to try and destabilize. They will continue to eat away at the edges by fomenting havoc with all the newly formed countries in that region."

She shook her head. "Damn good thing you work for our side, Murdoch. This is black ops stuff."

"Well," he hedged, rising and dusting off his hands, "I had to know, Dallas."

"Why?"

"Because I don't want to lose you."

Her heart bounded, reacting to the sudden emotion in his low tone. It was his eyes, however, that gave him away. Dallas saw the love shining in them—for her. Gulping, she said, "I guess that's a good reason."

"Want me to come along? I'll even pack your bags—and mine."

She grinned belatedly as he smiled. Holding out her hand, she said, "Come and sit with me."

"An offer I can't refuse." Murdoch ambled over and settled beside her. Wrapping his arm around her shoulder, he drew Dallas against him. As he kissed her mussed hair, he whispered, "Well? Can I crawl into your luggage and come along? Did you know I speak excellent French? The secret base will be in the French-speaking part of Switzerland. I could come in handy, you know, if you need a translator."

Chuckling, Dallas eased back enough to catch the glint in his eyes. "You are such a tease, Murdoch."

"But you love me anyway?"

Silence hung between them.

Dallas moistened her lips, which still held the taste of him. "I don't know when it happened, Mike. The first day, I really didn't like you. But now…"

"The first day was bad," he agreed, holding her warm gaze. "I love you, Dallas. I don't know when it happened, either, but you rubbed off on me." Lifting his hand, he swept a few silky strands of hair off her brow. "And if you say no, I'm coming anyway. Dane said you were going to need a good ops coordinator. You don't know this, but I have lots of training in that department. So I'm coming along no matter what you say." He flashed his teeth in a broad smile.

Laughing lightly, Dallas shook her head. "You really are incorrigible, Murdoch. Yes, I'd love to have you come along. Because I love you." There, the words were out. Dallas had waited so long to say that to a man. The last time she had, the Peruvian medical doctor had left her. She didn't think Mike would. And seeing the pleasure in his face, the joy in his eyes, her heart soared with happiness.

"That sounds right to me," he growled, and leaned down to kiss her smiling mouth. Her lips were wonderfully soft, and hungry once more. Resisting temptation, he eased back and said, "I have a special surprise for you when we get home to my apartment."

Groaning, Dallas said, "Don't tell me. A turkey."

"Well, that's not all." He gave her a squeeze. Resting his chin on her head, he said, "I guess I can tell you now. It really won't spoil the surprise. I noticed a while back that you often wear small pink diamond earrings. I got in touch with my friends in Mexico, and they know a jeweler who creates one-of-a-kind wedding rings."

Dallas grunted and sat back, amazed. "You didn't."

"Yeah, I did. I had him make a channel setting of small pink diamonds for your engagement ring. I have it in a box back at the apartment. I was going to give it to you for Christmas dinner dessert."

She saw the pride in his face. "I'll bet it's beautiful. I can hardly wait to see it. I love pink diamonds."

"You're the diamond in my life. In a couple of hours, we'll be home, darlin'. You're going to live with me until we get reassigned. The C.O. is going to miss us, but he'll get replacements. My life is with you—wherever they send you in this world of ours."

Reaching up, Dallas kissed Mike tenderly, then framed his face with her hands. "You know what you are to me?"

"Beside a huge pain in the ass at times?"

She remained sober. "I love your humor, Mike. But to me, you're my forever man."

He grasped her hands and held them. "Count on it, Dallas. But only if you'll be my forever woman."

She met his warm gaze, her heart melting. "Forever, Mike."

* * * * *

Don't miss Lindsay McKenna's next romance,
DANGEROUS PREY, available
December 2008 from HQN.

SNOWBOUND WITH A PRINCE

Susan Grant

For Eileen Nauman, extraordinary writer, woman and wonderful friend.

And to all the men and women in the armed forces serving overseas this Christmas and every day of the year— thank you for your service.

Prologue

Prince Aleksas aimed a bleary-eyed glare outside the VIP terminal at Virsland International Airport. He was at the parking spot that should have held one of his Porsches, or the new Ferrari.

"Where the hell is my car?" he mused out loud. Where was his entourage, for that matter? Alek had spent most of his life as the king of Virsland's sole heir, shaking off assistants and body-guards and countless other meddling staffers. Now when he needed them, they were nowhere to be found.

His Ferragamo boots clapped against the polished birch floors as he stalked back and forth in front of the exit doors, expecting that at any moment, someone would pull up in a sleek sedan, full of apologies, and offer him a ride home to the palace. The VIP terminal was utterly deserted. Granted, it wasn't used much, but there should have been a few people around. Even the nervous man who'd escorted him here from the main passenger terminal had vanished as well. Odd…and annoying as hell. Only midday, it was already twilight. In the dead of winter in Virsland the day was as bright as it was going to get. He should be sitting by a warm fire, a heavy crystal glass of excellent brandy in his hand, not prowling an empty airport terminal like any average person off the street.

He pulled out his cell phone. The battery was dead. Swearing, he shoved it back in his pocket. How could he be expected to keep up with such mundane details like charging phones? He was the crown prince. He had people to do that for him. People who weren't here. Damn them. "Damn everyone!"

His shout reverberated off the marble and glass walls. The empty terminal was a marvel of Scandinavian architecture. Right now it just seemed cold. Unwelcoming. Father should have allowed him a vacation before summoning him home, presumably to be scolded once again for not performing up to expectations. Alek refused to be held accountable. He'd never asked to be a military pilot, but Father insisted he take training at the Americans' base in Texas. Well, they'd kicked his ass out the door and sent him home. What did his father think would happen?

And so instead of passing a lazy day in a blissful daze on a remote tropical island where no one would demand or expect anything of him and where pleasure of every sort was a finger-snap away, he was here—bored, exasperated and alone.

"I need a drink!" Turning slowly, he searched for another human being to do his bidding. Anyone would do. "A shot of vodka for His Majesty the Crown Prince!"

All the bars were closed at this early hour.

He scrubbed a hand over his face. It was too damn early to be awake. To be conscious. It reminded him too much of the past six months he'd spent in pilot training: every morning up at dawn, dressed in his flightsuit and ready for the daily briefing, five days a week. He'd played the game as Father wanted him to—a favor, for the man was fighting cancer and no one knew if he'd win the battle—and it still wasn't good enough. Alek was never going to be the man his father needed him to be. When would the old man accept it? Maybe this time.

Alek dug in his pocket for a cigarette, then remembered he'd given up the habit during his months in Texas. His foul mood darkened. He wanted out of here—now. Almost a full day trapped in the first-class cabin of a commercial airliner from Dallas to Washington to London to Virshagen had left him feeling like a caged animal, even if the whiskey was top-notch, and even if the London flight attendant had pressed her phone number into his hand while he'd slept off the effects of the expensive alcohol. She, on the other hand, wouldn't have been expensive. The Fionas and Tatianas of the world never were. They came easy like everything else in his life. "Playboy," his critics called him. "The Heartbreak Prince." Alek shrugged. Could he help it if sweets fell so easily into his hands? Besides, he liked easy. Anything more required too much damn effort.

You'd have made the effort for Kathryn.

He came to a complete stop. His breath caught with a vision of the gorgeous, curly-haired, freckled little Texan with the big spirit and the even bigger heart, big enough for everyone, even him. He'd fallen for USAF pilot Kathryn Wallace the moment he saw her, the same moment that she more or less told him to go to hell.

"Hell-Kat," her squadron-mates called her, and for good reason, although there was a sensitive spirit hidden beneath that armor, one he wished fate had allowed him time to properly discover. Even so, Kathryn Wallace was one of only two people in the entire world he'd call a friend. Vincent Soren was the other, and Alek hadn't seen him in God knew when. The man was a Raptor, a member of the elite, thousand-year-old Virsland palace guards. He'd served several years as one of Alek's personal guards and often a confidante. *Jah,* Kathryn and Vincent knew him, the real him, because he let them in. To everyone else, he was a stranger. He'd learned early that most people wanted something from him. They wanted to befriend his money or status, or the power he perceived he held. Not Vincent. And not Kathryn.

Kathryn... He wished she was here now. If she were in his arms, nothing much would matter. A shudder of yearning went through him as he thought of her mouth and how for so long he'd wanted a taste of those sweet, soft lips...and more. So much more. Even now, in the throes of his frustration and his defeat, he felt his body reacting to the mere thought of holding her. Just holding her. The attraction had been mutual—her eyes didn't lie—but to Kathryn his character mattered more than his appearance. Character that was obviously lacking. Now he'd never see her again, and he doubted she was sorry.

Fool, she was too good for you. You damn well proved it, too. Into his mind flashed the scene of the military officials at the review board convened to get rid of him. All of the American officers wore their stiff, you-left-us-no-choice faces except for Kathryn. She'd appeared so sad and disappointed in him. He'd disappointed people all his life, but it never mattered until that moment.

"You're a born leader, Alek," she told him a few days earlier after his last training ride, observing him with those wide-open, utterly honest blue eyes that won his heart the instant he'd first looked into them. *"People believe in you even when you give them no damn reason. It's a gift, Alek, a God-given gift. Instead of lifting yourself into something worthy of their respect and loyalty, you act like you don't care. I think you do care. But you're not sure you're good enough. You work hard at making sure you're not. Then you don't have to worry about destroying anyone's expectations."*

Good God, he'd thought, sitting there across the table from her in the briefing room. That was exactly what he'd been doing all his life, running from having to find out if he measured up. It was as if a light had been shined on his soul, revealing the reason behind so many of his actions—or lack of action, which was often much worse. Instead of acknowledging she was right, he automatically sought refuge behind his "whatever" face. A model he used to date coined the term to describe the look of bored indifference he'd taken a lifetime to perfect. Whatever. *Jah*, it fit.

It didn't work on Kathryn, though. Never one to take his attitude, she walked out on him, slamming the briefing room door in his face. Even now, days later, the sound wouldn't leave his mind, that door banging closed over and over in the aching recesses of his brain with each beat of his pulse.

He swore bitterly as remorse tightened his gut. Frantically, he rooted in his pocket for a smoke. Again, he remembered he'd given up the habit. No cigarettes to distract him, no booze to blunt the ache of self-disgust. *You let Kathryn down.*

She could go to hell for all he cared. What right did she have to believe in him? Was it his fault she mistakenly assumed he was capable of more than what he was? Alek threw his arms out to the sides. "This is all there is, Kathryn, darling!" he called out. "This is it."

He fell into a leather chair, his long legs sprawled as he glowered outside at a panorama of snow-covered, forested hills. The familiar beauty soothed his dreadful temper. He might do his level best to shrug off the demands of being home, but the forest was in his blood and in his soul. No matter where in the world he tried to hide, the scents and sights of his homeland curled through his consciousness, subtly, seductively, calling him back.

Damn genes. He couldn't rid himself of his DNA any more than he could his royal title courtesy of one of the oldest, unbroken lines of royalty in the world, second only to Denmark's, originating in the time of Beowulf with a man called Haldor the Fierce. An ancient painting of the king, the oil paint cracked and darkened with age, hung in the Hall of Ancestors at the palace.

It terrified Alek as a child when he'd peer out at Haldor from the shadows. Yet, he was inexplicably drawn to the painting. Some said it was because he resembled the raider king. Alek spent many a long moment trying to see it for himself. Dressed in furs and armor, King Haldor sat on his throne with his hounds at his boots, glaring back at Alek, daring him, challenging him to live up to his destiny.

Alek snorted. He'd bet old Haldor never had to answer to people telling him what to do and when to do it. He'd never had to worry about public image or responsibilities. Or tabloids. And paparazzi.

"I think you do care."

Alek winced at the memory of her words. Perhaps that was why he never told Kathryn of his feelings for her before he left. He was afraid. He was so sure she'd find him inadequate that he'd let the opportunity slip away.

You're afraid... Haldor chimed in, his imagined voice rumbling and deep and slightly mocking. *Don't come back to me, boy, until you know the difference between a life wasted and a life spent.*

"To hell with you all!" Alek threw his cell phone across the waiting area. It shattered into pieces. His life was in the same state, and he hadn't a clue or even the motivation to cobble it back together. He was too far behind the eight ball, as the Americans would say.

A shadow moved across his vision. Oh, joy. Finally. His ride home was here—

Sudden pain seared his neck, cinching down and cutting off his air supply. He was lifted by whatever was wrapped around his neck and dragged backward off the chair. The chair fell over. His boots scraped over the floor as he tried kicking back onto his feet. Can't breathe. Sputtering, he clawed at his neck, felt leather-clad knuckles and a wire.

Blood pounded behind his eyes and in his head. A wild few glances told him there was more than one attacker. The others seemed to be milling around watching the spectacle. All of them were in plain clothes, black clothes, like what special agents in the Virs army wore. But his vision quickly dimmed, going from red to gray to black.

"Don't kill him," he heard someone warn.

The pressure around his neck eased. His vision returned. He rolled onto his hands and knees, grasping at his neck. His head felt half-severed. Blood, warm and slick dribbled over his hand and to the floor. The wire had cut deep.

"Vanhanen doesn't care if he stays pretty, does he?"

General Vanhanen? The commander of the Virsland military? Was this a coup? The men gave him no time to think about it. The boot that drove into his face ended all higher thought.

He'd always been athletic, agile, but his traveling clothes, jetlag, hangover and shock were no match for this out of the blue vicious attack. Instinctively, he tried to protect his head and face and gut, in that order. Someone grabbed his hair, yanking him into a more vulnerable position. "Worthless garbage," someone muttered and hit him again. "You won't be so pretty to the girls any longer, not that there'll be any where you're going." Laughter. Another powerful kick, this time in the groin.

Why the hell didn't he pass out? It seemed a cruel twist that he'd stayed conscious through the beating. Was it a strength of his ancestors passed down to him without his consent like everything else they gave him that he didn't want, like his royal blood? If there was ever a time he wanted to be a weakling and die, this was it. He'd hit rock bottom anyway. Why keep living? There was nowhere to go but lower. Might as well end it this way. It'd be good fodder for gossip if nothing else: *Crown Prince found in a bloody pulp in airport. Cleanup took hours.*

After a while, the blows blended together. His agony-fueled daze made it impossible to tell how much time had passed between the first blows and now. His nasal passages were swollen nearly shut. Blood ran down the back of his throat. One eye was so puffed-up he couldn't see out of it. The other eye was too blurred to make much sense of what he was looking at anyway. "Don't kill him," he was certain he heard a second time. The men rolled his worthlessly limp body in what felt like a Turkish rug. He was lifted and carried outside, judging by the faintest change in temperature, then dropped into a car. He sensed the pressure change when the trunk closed.

He wanted to die, but something in him fought to stay alive, kept him sucking in breath after breath when he felt as if he were suffocating, and damn well wanted to.

A blast of cold water woke him from a stupor. He'd been unrolled from the carpet. Men held his arms to keep him upright and on his feet. His head hung low. Blinking, he noted that blood had made interesting splash patterns on the white marble floor. His blood.

His floor.

They'd brought him to the throne room of the thousand-year-old winter palace in Virshagen. It was the main location of the government under one of the few monarchies in the world that still ran the country. To his left was a view of the Baltic Sea. In the midnight hour it glittered with hundreds of vessels. Every king since Haldor's time had enjoyed that view. Alek could barely see it through his swollen eyes. The lights of the city and the ships blurred and spun, doubling, tripling...

Another bucketful of ice water hit him in the face.

"You damn near killed him," a familiar voice scolded.

Sputtering, Alek choked on water and blood. "I'm awake, damn you!"

He struggled to lift his head. It felt as if it weighed a hundred pounds. "Welcome home," the voice said.

Alek swung his gaze in that direction. "Vanhanen," he

growled. The general was resplendent in his Virsland Royal Army dress greens. His epaulets and war medals sparkled. This was his father's trusted general for the last forty years. "What the hell are you doing on my father's throne?"

"Keeping you off of it. The time for the people has come. Listen to them, Aleksas."

The balcony doors were flung open, allowing in tangy sea air and a rumble other than the roar of the sea. People were chanting, yelling—a large crowd, Alek judged. What were they saying? Half deafened by blows to his head, he couldn't make out the words.

"Do you hear them? They're cheering," Vanhanen said. "I have declared a new government, beginning today."

"A military takeover? Are you kidding me? The people will never accept this."

"The uniform comes off once I am sworn in as president."

Surely, Vanhanen would not get away with this. The Barons family was loved by all. Weren't they? Alek knew there were ongoing problems with the economy since his father's illness. He remembered hearing some such thing, but he hadn't paid much attention. Maybe he should have.

"I promised the people a new future, Aleksas."

"*Prince* Aleksas."

"No more. The Barons represent the past, and it is time to cut ties with the past." Vanhanen addressed him gently, condescendingly, as if he were still a child.

Could he blame the man? After all, he'd acted like a child—irresponsible, living for pleasure. Letting down those he loved. Now, thrust into the middle of a military coup, he didn't know what to say, or how to act, or what to do to change its course. Whatever he'd come up with wouldn't be good enough. So he stood there, held by the guards, hiding behind his mask of indifference.

"You're a born leader, Alek."

No, Kathryn. I am not.

His head hung low. He almost passed out again. Pain and shock made him drift in and out of the nightmare that was reality, and the one that was his own rotting conscience.

"Aleksas…"

He head jerked up at the sound of his name being called in a very weak voice. Father's voice. He spun his gaze around in time to see his father being pushed down to his knees in front of Vanhanen and his army officers. No raptors, he thought. No palace guards. It gave him hope that the ancient royal guard had not defected, had not betrayed their king. He did recognize a few parliament members standing in the gathering, and hot rage began to boil. Traitors. How many others were in on this conspiracy? How long had they plotted, while his father fought his cancer and endured chemotherapy…*while you played?*

Alek's throat hurt too much to allow him a gulp of shame. He couldn't recall ever seeing his father kneel outside of church, and since Alek had avoided going to mass for years, the memory was fuzzy at best. Now his sire was crouched in front of the throne on which he should have been sitting. They hadn't beaten him like they had Alek, thank God. Alas, they didn't need to subdue him; the cancer had done it for them. The once-vibrant man's skin was chalky. He'd lost his hair. He was a ghost. An ousted king who'd tried to make a man out of his only heir, his one living blood relative. There should have been more heirs, *jah,* more siblings after Alek, boys and also girls, but King Christoffer never touched another woman after his wife, Alek's mother, was killed in an auto accident. Despite all the urgings of advisors and all the willing beauties, the king spurned making any more heirs, pinning all his hopes and dreams on Alek.

And Alek panicked. He couldn't bear the pressure. What if he was inadequate? He pretended to be weak. Stupid. His father knew better, and pushed him harder, waiting patiently for him to wake up. Putting his entire kingdom at risk, waiting for Alek to grow up and assume responsibility. God, it was all so clear now. Why had it taken him so long to see it? For fifteen years it had been just the two of them. All Alek had done was run from him, rebelling against everything, for he hadn't wanted to risk disappointing him. Yet, in the not wanting to, he had.

"You named your boat 'No Consequences'. Well, you were wrong. There are consequences, Your Highness."

With Kat's accusation ringing in his ears, Alek forced himself to meet his father's eyes. "I've failed you," he whispered. His father simply shook his head and glanced away—in disgust? In defeat? Alek tried to jerk his arms out of the guards' grip. "Father, I am—" *Sorry,* he meant to say, but a gunshot interrupted his apology. His father sagged to his side, blood pooling on the white marble like blood on virgin snow.

Alek bellowed in pain, then at Vanhanen. "You shot the king. You shot the king!" None of the men in the room spoke. Some seemed as shocked by the execution as Alek was.

His father's eyes were still open, the life not drained out of them yet as he seemed to stare at Alek in surprise. His sire's last moments of life would be spent watching his good-for-nothing son sniffling in the grip of guards.

"What will you do, son? What will you do now?" The question came in Haldor's voice, his father's voice—or his own; Alek wasn't sure. He saw the same question in Vanhanen's smirking eyes.

I will fight! Growling, Alek wrenched from the men's grip, kicking their legs out from under them. He may have acted spineless and stupid in the past, but he remembered the countless hours spent training him in martial arts, the only part of his education he'd paid any attention to. He wasn't any less afraid, no; but he'd fight for his father's honor and their kingdom despite the fear. Perhaps that was what courage meant, not the absence of fear but the triumph over it. A realization too late? Likely so, *jah,* but if he was going down, he'd go down fighting. These traitors had underestimated him just as he'd underestimated himself all these years.

In full sight of his dying father, in full view of the paintings of Haldor and the other kings and queens hanging in the Hall of Ancestors, Alek roared as he lunged forward, charging toward Vanhanen.

The scene played out in slow motion. With a glare as cold as the Baltic sea in January, Vanhanen swung the pistol around and aimed it at Alek's head. Behind the general was the sea, sparkling with ships in the night. Timeless. Eternal. "The future is now," the general said, and fired.

Chapter 1

Six years later

Strike two. USAF Captain Kathryn Wallace frowned at the receiver in her hand and hung up the telephone. After two tries she was still a "no-go" reaching Texas from Spain. The coldest and snowiest weather in recorded history had played havoc with communication throughout Europe, but she wasn't giving up on her phone call home, not yet. With images of the unfolding disaster playing on the news 24-7, her family would be worried about her flying as a C-17 pilot delivering humanitarian aid to some of the millions of people who so desperately needed it. After the hell her parents had suffered the past year, the horrible loss none of them had yet gotten over, the last thing she wanted was them losing sleep over her welfare. Just a few words to let them know she was safe were all she needed.

Kat dialed again and crossed her fingers, waiting for the line to open up. Maybe the third time would be the proverbial charm. As a last resort, she could try e-mailing, but with her sister-in-law and nephew visiting her parents' small farm, it wasn't likely the computer would get turned on, and definitely not late on a Sunday afternoon, Texas time. Mom and Dad were as stubbornly low-tech as a couple could be. Then again, they were farmers; they lived by sunrise and sunset and the weather. YouTube, iPod, cell phone—you might as well be speaking Mandarin Chinese.

Come on, come on. Ring! With the phone pressed to one ear and her finger stuck in her other, Kat tried to isolate herself from the hustle and bustle of transiting aircrews and support personnel consuming the base operations building at Morón Air Base. There was more tense energy in the air than usual. Not knowing when or if an individual mission would launch kept everyone on edge.

A large map of Europe dominated the opposite wall. Kat's impatient gaze tracked along the route of flight she'd be taking from Spain to the Baltic Sea then across the water, headed northeast. Virsland. It was a Northern European Monaco, a small, almost mythical kingdom with a violent past at odds with its fairy tale like reputation. Their resistance movement during World War II was so fierce that the Nazis never could crush them. The Brothers and Sisters were some of the bravest freedom fighters in history, winning the respect of the Allies, who, because of them, refused to give Virsland over to the Soviets when Europe was divvied up after the war.

Of all the countries in the world, she'd been assigned to deliver aid to this one. No one would ever guess that she, a Texas girl, once knew Aleksas Barons, Crown Prince of Virsland. Their paths never would have crossed if Alek hadn't been sent packing to the United States for pilot training. Kat and everyone she knew had fought tooth and nail for the chance to earn a pair of coveted silver air force wings. Alek had it handed to him on a platter like everything else in his life. But for one memorable summer and fall he brought glamour and excitement to remote Laughlin Air Force Base where she'd been stationed as an instructor pilot, captivating her despite her better judgment.

At the controls of a jet, Alek won her respect, but only there. Outside the cockpit, he was incorrigible, a pedigreed stray tomcat, a man who had it all and knew it, and yet whose easy charm and generosity attracted more friends than enemies. You wanted to hate him but couldn't. Now she'd finally see Alek's homeland, a fairy tale land of spire-topped castles and dense forests, fjords and charming fishing hamlets, snowy peaks and alpine meadows.

"This is my country…" The words burst inside Kat's mind in a seductive, breath-stealing baritone. *"This is beauty…"* It was as if Alek himself had spoke in her ear.

The memory swept her back to a collectibles store she used to frequent in Del Rio, Texas. She'd been browsing for a Christmas present for Kelly, her sister-in-law, when an antique snow globe caught her eye. She'd held it up to the light to admire it. Alek walked in off the street which was a popular stop on the way home from the base. Never seeming to be able to pass up the chance to talk with her, to tease her, to flirt with her, or to tell her a story, he'd spotted her and followed her inside. Fresh from his training classes, the prince had been dressed in a flightsuit that hung like a sack on everyone else but covered his broad shoulders and the tall, lean contours of his body with almost sinful perfection. The uniform had been custom-made from scratch by royal tailors, like almost everything else he wore on or off duty. Green and white fabric epaulets covered his shoulders: Virsland rank, further reminder of who he was. As always, his unique scent drifted around him: sweet yet masculine and a little bit spicy. No one smelled like Alek did, not then, not since.

"Ah…look!" He'd taken the snow globe from her hand and gave it a shake. White flakes swirled around a tiny village surrounded by miniscule tress and cows. "This is my country," he'd said. "This is Virsland."

The pride in his voice and his obvious homesickness touched her. She knew that it showed in her gaze. Alek's voice dropped lower as he searched her eyes, her face. "This is beauty…"

For a giddy moment she almost believed he meant that *she* was beautiful. She'd blushed even as she hated how he could play her like he played so many women.

The memory left Kat's skin tingling and her blood running hot. Softly, she swore, realizing where she was—hanging on to a pay phone at an air force base in Spain in the middle of the night. Not in Del Rio. Not inches from Alek Barons. Didn't matter, though; he had the same effect on her now all these years later as he did then. Time hadn't dimmed the anger.

Or the attraction. An image of handsome Alek throwing back his head in laughter filled her mind. Her father always told her that you could tell a lot about a man's true character by the quality of his laugh and how he treated his dog. Alek's laugh was wholehearted, slightly husky and unmistakably real. That laugh was part of his can't-hate-him appeal. He could break a girl's heart and leave her feeling good about it.

Not Kat's heart. Never hers. She had never let him anywhere near it.

Often she wondered if that had been a mistake.

Wincing, she pulled her gaze from the map. She didn't want to think of Alek. But did she really expect she'd be able to think of Virsland without remembering that impossibly cocky and arrogant man, that hugely talented man who refused to see his potential and all he could have been? By birth, Aleksas Barons was an aristocrat and a warrior. By destiny, a leader, a statesman, a king. Problem was, he viewed that destiny as a life sentence he couldn't get lifted. He once confided how much he despised and resented being born for a single, "prepackaged" purpose.

Mistaking bad choices for freedom, he rebelled against it. In reality, he'd rebelled against himself. By twenty-four, his past resembled the front page of a tabloid. He'd dated starlets and heiresses, crashed expensive cars. He'd even fathered an out-of-wedlock child from a liaison with a drug-addicted supermodel when he was only seventeen, which made him only sixteen at the time of conception. Not that fatherhood slowed Alek down any. He'd partied his way through his teen years and into his twenties. Not once did Kat ever remember hearing him acknowledge that he had a son.

Alek's military service was supposed to have been a bridge and a rite of passage from reckless youth to responsible adulthood. It seemed to work for other princes, like Harry and William and Frederik. Not Alek. At Laughlin, the prince's carousing was the stuff of legends. Yet, despite late nights and God knew what else, Alek was one "hot stick." He could fly rings around most of the other students. It was a testament to his raw talent as a pilot seeing that he never cracked a book as far as Kat could tell, leading him to ace all his flights but fail all his written tests, which, of course, didn't concern him at all. Alek approached life with an utter disregard for consequences. Well, consequences he got—in spades—from her, from the US Air Force and from the people in his own kingdom. Watching the news of the coup and seeing the violence that followed, she'd often wondered at what point it hit him that his charmed existence was over.

She glanced out a frosted-over window and shivered but not from the cold. She hoped that at least Alek died well. Bravely. Somehow she knew he had. He was trouble, a bad boy in the truest sense, but he wasn't weak.

Damn you, Alek. You had so much potential, and you threw it all away. She gripped the telephone receiver until her fingers throbbed. Dead, the man still infuriated her! From the day she met him until the day he left the base, he drove her crazy—

The phone jerked out of her hand. Only then did she realize she'd been pacing and wandered too far from the phone's base. She snatched the dangling receiver out of the air and pressed it hard against her ear in hopes of hearing the call when it finally connected.

"Un momento, por favor."

Kat jumped at the voice. It took a second to realize a Spanish operator was speaking to her. "Yes, yes, I'll wait. No problem."

Static hissed and the call went through.

"Hello?" Kat hoped they could hear her. "Hello?"

A whoop of delight pealed from the other end of the phone line. "Everyone, it's Aunt Kat!"

She grinned at her nephew's excitement. Hearing Liam act like the animated little boy he used to be before his father's death was a special joy. There had been too many sad days since losing Mack, her twin brother, in Iraq. "How are you, my main man?"

"We're eating dessert! Mom made brownies."

"Chocolate chip?"

"Yeah."

"Not long now and I'll be eating brownies with you. And giving you an Aunt Kat hug. You'd better be ready for a big squeeze."

That won her a few more precious giggles. She hadn't seen Liam since her twin brother Mack's burial. Eleven months of duty had kept her away. This Christmas, though, it would take an act of war to keep her from her spending two weeks' leave in Dallas, Texas, with the rest of her tight-knit family. Kelly, her sister-in-law, kept telling her how important it was for Liam that Kat be home for the holidays. Ever since Mack was killed in action, Liam fretted with a child's insecurity that Kat, too, would perish. It broke her heart. Kat knew her risks were far lower than those her twin had faced. He'd been a Marine engaged in ground combat; she flew C-17 cargo planes. He'd been stationed in Iraq; she flew around the world from Antarctica to Peru, now even Virsland, but nowhere that qualified as a genuine hotspot. The

C-17 was too valuable a target to risk. If anything looked iffy, the air force sent along Ravens: two to six soldiers with big-ass guns—M-4s and attitude. Heck, she felt safer in her C-17 than at a fast food drive-through. Hers was a totally different situation from what Mack's had been, but try telling that to a worried seven-year-old who lost his greatest hero just two weeks after Christmas last year. "I'm doing great, Liam. I'm having a lot of fun. Tell everyone. Tell them not to worry."

"Aunt Kat's having fun, and she says she's not worried," her nephew cried to the family she knew was gathered around the table for Sunday dinner: pot roast slow cooked with barbeque sauce, mashed potatoes, canned home-grown green beans, a big cold pitcher of sweet tea—she could almost taste it. She smiled at the din of her family calling out that they missed her and loved her. No one dared take the phone from Liam.

"Are you in Virsland yet?" he asked in his thin little voice.

"Not yet, sweetie. We're waiting for the weather to clear up."

"I saw all the snow on TV! Mom says it's even snowing in Africa."

Gibraltar, technically, but it showed just how unusual the weather was. Even here in Spain it was sub-zero and had been for weeks. People were starving and freezing to death, even in the cities. Some said it was new ice age. If so, Kat figured she'd better invest in much thicker long underwear. She was a Dallas girl; the cold had settled into her bones and stayed there. "We'll wait for a hole in the clouds," she explained in simple terms, sensing concern behind his questions. "As soon as it opens up, we'll deliver warm clothes and food to the people in Virsland. They get an early Christmas."

"Then you're coming home, right?"

"Just like I promised." Static disrupted the line. She was about to lose the call. "Liam, you still there?"

"Yes!"

"What do you want me to say to Santa when I see him?" It was said the legend of Santa Claus sprang to life in snowy, forested Virsland. The Virslanders needed Santa now; that was for sure. "What do you want for Christmas?"

Silence met her question. For a panicked moment she feared he might ask for Mack. Had the boy been a few years younger, likely he would have. Kat knew he was thinking it. Her eyes started to fill. "Cookies," Liam said finally.

Kat swallowed a lump in her throat. "Just cookies?"

"Real Santa's cookies. From Virsland."

"Okay, sweetie. Santa's cookies. You got it."

Kat hung up and wiped the back of her hand across each eye. *Mack, on Christmas morning you, me and Liam are gonna dip those Santa cookies in hot chocolate. I know you'll be there with us in spirit.* She kept her back toward the busy hallway, breathing deep to steady herself as she held the cool metal squares of Mack's dog tags in her fist. They'd made red marks on her palm. She hadn't realized she'd gripped the tags so tightly during the phone call. Since the tags arrived in a too-small box filled with some of Mack's possessions last January, courtesy of his wife, Kelly, Kat never flew without them. They were always around her neck or in her hand. She needed a tangible reminder of Mack's memory; she needed it under her skin like a sliver. Then it didn't feel so much like half of her was missing.

She'd spent last Christmas assigned to the Peruvian operation with the Black Jaguar Squadron, losing her last chance to see her brother. She'd volunteered for the mission, figuring she had years of Christmases ahead to make up for being apart for this one.

Now she knew better.

If not for meeting Dallas Klein in Peru, an amazing, kick-ass pilot who like most Israelis knew her way around loss, Kat might have let grief bring her to her knees. Over drinks in a bar in Lima, the pilot had offered a supportive shoulder when Kat needed it most. They became fast friends. It was fate—after all, the woman was named after her hometown. The last e-mail Dallas sent had arrived from hot and dusty Arizona. The weather couldn't be more different from here.

Kat tucked the dog tags into her flightsuit. *I'll be there with your kid, Mack. I'll be there Christmas morning.*

"Captain Wallace!" The meteorologist held a fistful of weather printouts. Next to the tech sergeant was a full colonel and a civilian in a standard government suit. This was serious business; they'd brought in the experts to help. "We've got ourselves a break in the weather. It's a narrow window. If you're going to launch, now's the time."

"We're on our way." Once more Captain Wallace, aircraft commander, she took the printout, scanning the data as the men briefed her. Pulling temporary duty in Christchurch, New Zealand, working Operation Deep Freeze with runs down to Antarctica had taught Kat all about operating within defined "windows" of good weather. With three C-17s scheduled in and only one allowed on the ground at a time it would be tight, though. As long as there was enough fuel to fly a holding pattern high above the airfield until the moment was right, a coordinated triple land-unload-take off could happen.

She'd make it happen. With Christmas only a week away, and a promise made to a little boy, she wasn't getting stuck out anywhere.

Briefed by the meteorologists, Kat turned crisply on her heel and strode away. It was time to gather up her crew.

Chapter 2

Kat found her crew scattered around the couch and chairs in the lounge amongst discarded candy wrappers and soda cans. "Folks, it's clearing out up north. Not for long, though. Let's boogie."

Everyone was instantly alert, tossing the trash, gathering their stuff. The copilots were here, the loadmasters, too, but no Ravens. The airfield was secure: Virsland had its problems with an increasingly unpopular government but it wasn't considered a hostile area. No one was protesting now, anyway; they were too busy trying to keep warm. Since it was a relief mission and no attack was expected, only she and the senior load, Staff-Sergeant Manny Williams—"Luau"—would carry arms: 9 mm semi-automatic pistols, Berettas. Still, she was glad it was an augmented crew: double of everything with two copilots, two loadmasters, and, waiting outside in the maintenance hangar, a single crew chief to take care of any repairs on the ground in Virsland. No one wanted the C-17 breaking down in this kind of weather, especially her.

Kat's copilots, Lieutenants Rachel Morales, a statuesque Latina bombshell, and Tom "Tombo" Nolan, a stocky red-head from Iowa with a gelled-up crew cut, donned their leather jackets to the sound of a newscaster's voice coming from the TV: "Military crews are working round the clock delivering humanitarian aid during Europe's coldest, snowiest winter since the ice age." Scenes showed the blizzard into which they were about to fly. Jarring was the sight of an icebreaker ship trapped in the frozen-solid Thames River. A frosted-over camera lens added to the gloomy sight.

"A break, huh?" Tombo pulled on an olive-green wool hat. "The weatherman's on drugs."

"His crystal ball says we're going to ride in between the two lows. The second low is supposed to be really low, like bottom-out low, but we'll be in and out before it gets bad."

That elicited more than a few grumbles about not wanting to be stranded in "the North Pole." It was sad in a way. Not too many years ago, Virsland was considered the jewel of the Northern Baltic. Few crews would have minded an overnight or two there: the gregarious, gorgeous locals, the warm and cozy bars, the vodka that could roll your socks down with a single sip. But that Virsland was gone, just as Alek was. Alek, dead. To this day a part of her refused to accept it. Almost seven years had passed since she first laid eyes on him, and it felt like yesterday. She and three instructor friends were cast adrift in a stalled-out ski boat. There they were in the middle of Lake Amistad in the middle of July in the middle of west Texas, awaiting a tow back to the marina. Kat had just handed out big, fat Mexican cigars to celebrate the birth of her nephew to her brother and his wife. To her friends' delight, she joined them. She'd never smoked a cigar in her life. It was as good a moment as any to try. Then Alek came to the rescue. His first impulse was always to help people. It was another reason it was nearly impossible to dislike him. Throttle

him, yes. Dislike, no. As if it were yesterday, she could still hear
the deep rumble of a finely tuned engine. If not for the unlit cigar
clamped between her teeth, her mouth would have fallen open
at the sight of the approaching boat. It was sleek and very obviously expensive....

*"No Consequences," Kat said, reading the craft's name.
"Hmm." It looked like it should be racing off the Côte d'Azure, not
in a man-made reservoir a few miles away from the Rio Grande.*

*"You have trouble?" the driver called to them in an accented
voice. Like his boat, he seemed ripped from the pages of a
decadent, glossy foreign-language magazine. An ear stud and the
tattoo on his upper arm screamed "bad boy" yet a gold cross
hung from his neck. Sinner more than saint, she suspected. His
deeply suntanned, athletic body gleamed with oil.*

*She'd never seen him before. He must be a new student—a
foreign student, based on the accent. A rich one, too.*

*"Engine's acting up," her friend Rocket shouted back. "Can
you tow us in?"*

*Rich Boy answered with a nod. There were two other men with
him—military, too, judging by their short hair—and three women
Kat recognized as local arm-candy, having seen them around
hooked up with various pilots. The prettiest one draped her arms
over his shoulders as she whispered something in his ear. Kat
gave her bikini top a self-conscious tug as the wind blew her
tangled curls across her face, causing her sunglasses to slide
down her nose, which had never lost its little-girl curve—or its
little-girl freckles.*

*Wheeling the über-boat around, Rich Boy shoved the throt-
tles forward, circling their shipwreck to the approving murmurs
of her friends. Then, chopping the power at the very last moment,
he coasted close, stopping precisely alongside them.*

"I hope he's got as much skill flying jets," she said.

One of the male passengers threw them a tow rope. Kat was

*on her knees helping Frank secure the line when residual wake
from Rich Boy's acrobatics knocked her sideways. She righted
herself, muttering, and tugged on her bikini top. Then she paused
to retie the halter strings, clenching the fat cigar between her
teeth for lack of hands or anywhere to put it.*

*A low and liquid voice spoke. "In my country, the women do
not waste time with bikini tops."*

*Hands behind her neck, Kat glared up from under her mop of
curls. His mouth twitched with amusement at the sight of the
cigar before his gaze slid down her bikini-clad body, assessing
and seeming to approve.*

*To her horror, Kat blushed. To her further horror, she realized
there was no way he'd missed her reaction. She gave her halter
strings one last yank and pulled the cigar from her mouth. "I take
it your women don't smoke cigars, either."*

"Indeed, they do not."

"Indeed," she mimicked, "your women are boring."

*There he stood, staring at her with a look of complete shock,
a glistening, six-foot-something Euro-god cut down to size by a
hundred-and-five-pound, freckle-nosed Texas girl. She figured
he'd make her swim to shore. Instead, he burst out laughing,
"Boring, the women in my country may be compared to you."*

"Now you're finally making sense."

*"Am I?" He slipped off his sunglasses as he extended his hand
and helped her aboard. His eyes were vivid hazel, a mix of moss
and silver. Designer, too? Her feeling was that they were the real
deal. He raised goose bumps on her arms with his gaze alone
despite the heat that day. She wanted to attribute her lighthead-
edness to the blistering sun and not him but couldn't.*

*She yanked on her bikini top, pushed on her sunglasses and
made her way to the aft seats on the boat.*

*When they arrived at the marina, she wasted no time jumping
out of the boat. Alek called out, "Wait." He reached up, caught*

her hand and drew her fingers to his mouth. Surprisingly warm and soft lips grazed over her knuckles. Her friends choked back their laughter. Oh, she was going to hear about this all day. No, all week. Shoot, by the time the story hit the officer's club bar on Friday, it would be totally blown out of proportion. "When will I see you again?" he asked.

The kiss may have been public, but his voice was low and intimate, his gaze intense and focused, as if there was only them and no one else. For a moment, there wasn't. She imagined that when he made love to a woman, he made her feel as if she were the only woman in the universe, the only woman for him. Until he moved on to the next one, that was.

"We'll see each other soon," she assured him. As in Monday morning, bright and early at the daily briefing. Poor man.

"But I don't even know your name."

"You can call me lieutenant." She watched the surprise spread over his handsome face. "Lieutenant Wallace."

Dropping that bombshell, she turned and walked away, asking herself why she was so hard on him.

Because she was attracted to him and didn't want to be.

It wasn't until she read a local newspaper that night that she learned the identity of the man who'd kissed her hand. Alek Barons was the Crown Prince of Virsland. Now it made sense. He made sense. Of course, the man radiated privilege. Of course he owned expensive toys. Prince Far-Too Charming. The man was a master flirt. Maybe she'd been just as guilty of flirting that day. Maybe because like his boat's name, there were no consequences to doing so. She couldn't follow up. She couldn't ask for his number or give him hers. She couldn't date him, or even hook up with him. The gulf between student and instructor was too wide. Professionally, she was bound to respect it.

Good thing she had. When she was called to testify at Alek's training review board months later she was able to do so without the distraction of impropriety. Maybe it was better Alek Barons was dead; he wasn't around to hate her for what she did.

In real life, the fairy tales didn't always have happy endings. Touching Mack's dog tags to ground her in the present, Kat pulled her thoughts out of the past. Her focus had to be here and now, firmly on the mission to help the people Prince Alek never survived to rule because of his damned immature shortsightedness. "Okay, let's move it, guys."

As a group, they exited the break area. Other crews still lounged around waiting for their relief missions to launch. If not for the conditions, planes would be flying around the clock. That they couldn't was a tragedy in progress. People needed the aid. Well, today Kat and her crew would do their part.

"Better snow than sand," Tombo said, tugging his wool hat over his ears. "Sand, I hate it. In Saudi it was sand, sand everywhere."

"How'd you get sand everywhere, Tombo?" A giggle accompanied Rachel's question.

"Wouldn't you like to know?"

"I do. I mean, really." She provoked Tombo like a little sister—a little sister who just happened to be one of the best and sharpest pilots in the squadron, and Tombo knew it. Rachel was one copilot Kat could rely on to truly run the airplane while she was on a break. Last month they flew a massively long mission from Dhaka, Bangladesh nonstop to Hickam Air Force Base— seventeen and a half hours long, with two air-to-air refueling sessions along the way. Kat had felt comfortable enough with Rachel up in the cockpit to take a nap between the refueling sessions. Some copilots weren't that trustworthy. But Rachel had made contact with the next tanker and set everything up before waking Kat.

"What does 'everywhere' mean, Tombo?" Rachel persisted.

"My ears. My eyes. And in my ass."

Rachel blushed. "How did you get sand in your—?"

"Rache." Kat made a slicing motion across her neck. It was hard to say if Tombo was irritated or entertained. Either way, Kat had a mission to run, and her crew was going to be focused on it, even if it meant playing "Mom." An aircraft commander wore many hats. Protector was another, Kat thought, thinking of her Beretta. Add strategist, drill sergeant, mediator, cheerleader and therapist to the list, too.

"Luau," she said to her senior loadmaster.

"Ma'am." He fell in step with her.

"If we don't get off the ground fast, the guys coming in after us can't land. Virsland's expecting us, but because of the conditions, I don't know what kind of help we're going to have when we get there."

"A fleet of K-loaders and forklifts would be nice." Sergeant Williams flashed his trademark killer grin. The big, good-looking Hawaiian got looks from women wherever he went. "And some hot soup."

Kat laughed. "I hope you're right." During relief operations most of the time there was host-nation help. It was up to the crew and the host-nation folks on the ground do their best in getting the job done.

"We've got it under control," he assured her. "Me and Steamer here will be ready to go the second those tires hit the tarmac."

Sergeant Clamm, aka "Steamer," nodded with enthusiasm. She'd never flown with the lanky loadmaster who with that blond crew-cut and a touch of acne looked barely out of his teens. She'd heard he was sharp. Luau and steamed clams, it was making her hungry.

They pushed past the doors leading out to the ramp and a wall of darkness and cold. It was the kind of night to be snuggled up under soft blankets, not outside pounding the tarmac. As she turned the corner to the van that would bring them to the plane, a wall of frigid air stole her breath. A Texas girl didn't belong here. In her world, ice was what you put in a pitcher of sweet tea in the summertime. You didn't walk on it, and you didn't try to breathe it in.

Kat turned her collar up against the wind and hunched down, desperately conjuring mental images of summertime in Dallas to keep her going: heat lightning, cicadas, thick, muggy evenings. Didn't make a difference. The dry cold cut through her flight jacket so fast it felt like she was wearing tissue paper underneath instead of long-johns. And it was only a taste of what waited for them up north in Virsland.

Chapter 3

Within the hour, their group of three aircrafts had been whittled down to two. Stuck on the ground with a maintenance problem, the crew of the third C-17 finally had to cancel once it became apparent they'd miss the window of good weather. "Godspeed, you guys," the aircraft commander radioed, wishing them luck. "And put in a good word with Santa for us."

The two C-17s pressed on through the night with their precious cargo. They watched the sun come up while flying turns in a holding pattern waiting for clearance into Virsland. Finally cleared for approach, they left the second C-17 to bore holes in the sky, waiting in holding for their turn to deliver the cargo.

A sigh of delight escaped Kat as the aircraft broke though the clouds on landing. Below and all around was a glorious panorama, a winter wonderland in the truest sense of the word. Forested hills surrounded the airport. Evergreens bowed under the weight of snow like a Christmas tree with too much flocking.

Picturesque villages dotted the countryside: clusters of gaily decorated roofs with an occasional church spire jutting higher. The capital city of Virshagen glimmered in the distance, closer to the sea. Snow flurries sparkled like glitter where the sun shone through breaks in the clouds.

Kat felt oddly overcome by emotion. The past year she'd felt adrift, a bit lost; getting over losing her twin brother had been even rougher than she'd expected. She'd been numb for so long that feeling anything other than grief was welcome. Soaring over Virsland, she felt a little more alive, a little more like the old Kat, and that was a damned miracle.

Rachel made a soft whistle as she stared out the cockpit windows. "It's like being in one of those snow globes."

This is my country…

"This *is* beauty, Rache," Kat murmured with a tremble that had nothing to do with the weather and everything to do with Alek Barons. "This is Virsland…"

Not the hell anymore, she corrected herself. Not without its king. *Not without you, Alek. Damn it, you belong here with your people.* Time hadn't dimmed the feeling that the world had lost something, that she'd lost something, when Alek died. The thought was too crazy to dare admitting it to anyone. Maybe even to herself.

After landing, Kat squinted at a scene of blinding white as she taxied the plane off the runway. Every aircraft and building in sight was sugar-coated. In fact, it was deadly ice. Seeing it up close turned what she'd heard in the news into reality.

Before they'd rolled fully onto the taxiway, Luau was on his way downstairs to the cargo area with a manifest of the goods they'd brought with them. They had no time to spare.

A follow-me truck met the plane at the runway exit. Flashing its lights, it led them toward the parking area, which, Kat noted with some dismay, wasn't anywhere near the small terminal. No quick dash-and-go for real-live "Santa cookies" for Liam. She'd be reduced to hitting the Morón BX when she got back unless another opportunity presented itself.

And it probably wouldn't. The airport appeared deserted. Snow drifted to the rooftops of some of the buildings. What planes weren't hangared were wing-deep in snow and coated with ice. Icicles longer and fatter than she'd ever imagined possible ran the length of the control tower. Several idling trucks and the group of men who waited to unload the cargo were the only signs of life— and even that was debatable. The group waiting for them was so bundled-up in cold weather gear that it was impossible to tell if they were male or female, civilian or military. Like somber snowmen, they radiated gloom. "Ho, ho, ho, Merry Christmas," Kat muttered.

"They don't look very merry," Rachel pointed out.

"That's what she's saying, Rache," Tombo said.

Kat shrugged. "What do we want them to do, I guess—wave signs? Cheer? It's thirty below—and today's a nice day."

"Nice?" Tombo snorted. "I'll never complain about Iowa in January again."

Kat pulled into the parking spot and stopped. They ran the shut-down checklist and secured the plane under the large Virsland People's International Airport sign. "*People's*. A little bit hypocritical. The more actual power dictators grab for them-selves, the more fictional power they allot to the *people*."

"I thought they had a president now," Rachel said as she stowed her approach plates. "They got rid of the monarchy."

"The president was an army general until the day of the in-auguration. He's been in office over six years so far with no election. He's a dictator in president's clothing."

"How do you know so much about this place?"

"The Prince of Virsland—the former prince—was a student when I was an instructor at Laughlin."

Rachel's brows went straight up. Alek's execution had only increased his glamour quotient, much like Princess Di's death had done with hers, although Alek's was a tarnished glamour. "Was he as bad as they say? Didn't he make a baby with Mira Truly, the supermodel, like, when he was sixteen?"

"Seventeen."

"Tragic that she overdosed, though. Stupid. She had so much going for her. She had a prince."

"I don't think they saw it that way, or at least I don't think Alek did. Knowing him, Mira was just another hook-up. That's just the way he was. You wanted to smack him for how he acted sometimes, but you couldn't. He had this addictive charm, Rache. It kept you coming back for more." Feeling silly, she stopped and cleared her throat.

"Did you ever fly with him?" Rachel persisted, not wanting to let it drop.

"Twice." Flying had been an excuse to be in close quarters with Alek, something barred by decorum almost everywhere else—and by her own fear that if they ever touched it would be spontaneous combustion and they wouldn't be able to stop. There were times when she'd catch him alone and watching her with such undisguised longing that she'd nearly said screw the rules, and screwed him. But at the speed Alek restocked his empty arms with ready and willing females she didn't fantasize for long that there could ever be anything real between them. To Alek life was just a game, and Kat was no man's toy. "I gave him the highest grade I could give. Rache, he had the ability to make the jet do anything he wanted, and with the kind of precision that made you want to weep with awe. But he couldn't pass the written tests. We begged him to study. No one wanted to send him home—it'd be an embarrassment for both countries—so he was allowed to stay in the program."

"Any other student would have been booted out on the street long before that."

"Exactly. I don't know if he ever knew or cared just how much we helped him behind the scenes. He took it for granted, I think. He took everything for granted. Since the day he was born people cut him slack and let him get away with whatever he wanted." Kat fiddled with a zipper on a leg pocket on her flight-suit. "Midway through the year, I upgraded to squadron check pilot. They chose me to give him his final review ride. I guess they figured they were giving him another break because I'd passed him with flying colors once before. They assumed I'd pass him again."

Rachel's eyes widened. "Omigod. You busted him. You washed Prince Alek out of pilot training."

"He washed his own flippin' self out, Rache."

Alek was sprawled elegantly in the chair across from her small briefing desk, rolling a pencil between long, blunt-tipped fingers. The papers she'd used to administer his oral exam after their sortie sat in a neat little pile. He'd gotten about every question wrong. "Alek, make me believe the language was a barrier or that something back home's got you distracted. You're worried about your father. Tell me that you didn't go out partying last night instead of sticking your head in the books—just this once—when it counted. Please. Give me something to use."

The door was closed; they were alone in the room. But her tone dropped lower nonetheless. Nerves made her pulse pound. She could get in a lot of trouble giving him this much leeway. Why put her career on the line for this pretty boy prince? Because he was so much more than…than this.

Because she was half in love with him.

He seemed restless, as if he ached to be somewhere else—on the lake, at the bar, in some woman's bed, anywhere but here. "I did not study, no. And for none of the reasons you proposed."

Damn it. He'd been out playing. He'd blown off his chance to stay here and graduate.

"But I flew a perfect Cuban eight, did I not? And that last landing—was it not sweet?" He smiled one of his smiles that made her tingle all the way down to her toes. It was as if he'd come to rely on his charm to make it all better. Well, it wouldn't make it better. Not this time.

"I can't pass you on the ride, Alek."

A small muscle jumped in his jaw, broadcasting his surprise. Unbelievable: Alek Barons was actually gobsmacked. It was the first indication that she'd gotten through to him.

"You named your boat 'No Consequences'. Well, you were wrong. There are consequences, Your Highness."

She gathered her belongings and stood. At the door, she stopped, taking a breath. How could she be doing this to him? Alek of all people. He remained sitting right where she'd left him, rolling that pencil.

He didn't even look up. She pushed open the door with a shaking hand and walked out.

Kat shoved her pilot's seat all the way back and unbuckled her seatbelt. In her line of sight was the gray and white façade of Virsland Airport, but in her mind she saw Alek standing in front of the panel of base officials a few days after that last, fateful ride together. Alek was dazzling in his Virsland dress greens, a white and gold ascot, forest green beret, and knee-high polished leather boots. The tiny earring in his left earlobe caught the harsh fluorescent light, sparkling. As the board read their decision, Alek's gaze found hers and lingered. He looked every inch the prince, but as he searched her face his eyes were bright with a combustible mix of regret and disgust.

He's sorry, she remembered thinking. Alek Barons had never appeared sorry about anything. He and guilt simply didn't cross paths. At times, she'd envied that. Imagine going through life never having to apologize. The disgust in his gaze, however, was unsettling. Was it directed at himself or her?

She never found out. A moment later he turned briskly on his heel and strode from the room. She never saw him again.

Rachel asked quietly, "Do you know how he died?"

"He was executed. I don't know any details. I don't think anyone does. Not a lot of news got out of Virsland around that time." For weeks afterward she'd combed every newspaper, watched every news show obsessively, searched for what she could on the Internet, and came up with nothing but nauseatingly over-the-top, this-is-a-new-day-for-Virsland speeches given by the new president, former military strongman Erik Vanhanen. There were clips of happy, cherubic tow-headed children frolicking in the snow, but no hint on what happened to the king, prince, or their cabinet. There had been blood spilled, but there was no sign of it. It was like history had been wiped clean of Alek Barons.

How did you die, Alek? Did you meet your end like the man I know you were? The question often consumed her. The answer was likely one she'd never have.

A rumble and a thump told Kat the cargo ramp had opened. The loadmasters were already at work. The temperature inside the cockpit plunged as the frigid air rushed in, even though the auxiliary power unit was providing heat.

Kat threw off her harnesses. "Keep it moving," she reminded Rache and Tombo. "I want us ready to launch the moment the cargo is off."

Leaving them to work on organizing the return leg, Kat bundled up in winter gear, armed herself with her pistol and climbed down to join the loadmasters to see where she could help. The rented parka was too large and allowed in cold air, but it would keep her warmer than her leather flight jacket. She'd need that warmth working in the cargo bay. Some aircraft commanders sat and watched the loadmasters do their job, or hung out upstairs in the cockpit loading the routes for the leg out and coordinating things like fueling. Not Kat. In her opinion, a good aircraft commander did all that during cruise on the way in or delegated it to the copilots in order to be free to go downstairs and share in the work ASAP, as she just had. Besides, off-loading got her out of the seat and counted as her exercise that day. Being a woman, especially, she gained credibility when she showed she could get her hands dirty pushing pallets. Plus, having more help expedited getting out of some not-so nice places quicker. Quick was what she needed today.

Kat paused with her gloved hands gripping the railing at the open side door. The air was so cold it felt like razors slicing the exposed skin on her face. Usually she walked to the cargo ramp outside the plane—it was quicker—but five seconds at the doorway convinced her to take the inside route. *Not so fast*—she released the railing but her gloves remained stuck to the metal. Now, that was cold. She jerked her hands away and managed to get free without ripping the gloves.

Through the cavernous plane she went, skidding to a stop as she nearly collided with the crew chief, Airman Chin.

"Ma'am," he said, breathless. "Luau sent me to get you."

"Hey, you'd better get a move on the walk-around." Kat wondered why he wasn't already outside checking the exterior of the aircraft. What could be going on below that was so important that Luau had to send him up instead of letting him do his job? "The weather's not going to hold for long, and the other plane's waiting to get in. We can't waste time."

"They won't let me outside."

"What do you mean? Who won't let you out?"

"The rampies. They're giving us a hard time about the cargo."

"Sergeant Williams has the manifest."

"They don't care." Vapor gusted out of Chin's nose with each breath in the dry, frigid air. "They want us to make some kind of statement. A written statement. In the terminal."

"Oh, I don't think so." Kat pushed past him to find out for

herself. She found Steamer pacing at the top of the open ramp
looking frustrated. A quick scan revealed that webbing had been
removed on some of the pallets, and at least one crate was rotated,
but that was all the progress the loadmasters had made. Usually
by this point, they'd be actively off-loading, helped by equipment
brought on by the ramp personnel at the airport. "Luau's down
there, Captain," the loadmaster told her. "They've ordered us to
vacate while they inspect the cargo."

"That's not going to happen." Overseas, US airplanes have the
same immunities accorded warships—immunity from search,
seizure *and* inspections. "I'm sure whatever's going on is just a
misunderstanding."

"I don't know, ma'am. They seem pretty upset."

Together, they shifted their attention to the group of Virslanders standing in a semicircle around Luau at the bottom of the
ramp. Frowning, the officials were bundled up so thickly in
parkas and Russian-style fur hats with ear flaps that Kat couldn't
tell what agency they belonged to, though their airport badges
seemed official enough. The shortest of the men waved the
manifest at Luau, yelling at the big Hawaiian in broken English.

Kat groaned. "I'll go patch things up." She strode down to the
tarmac. The icy air stung—both her body and her Texas sen-
sibilities. She yanked her collar higher around the face, tugging
down on her hood, retreating into the warmth like a turtle into
its shell. Did it have to be so flippin' cold?

Luau met her halfway. "Houston, we have a problem."

"That's what I gather. Chin and Steamer told me they want
us off the plane."

"Yeah, inside the terminal to answer questions about the
cargo. While we're doing that, they're going to have an inspector go through the crates."

"No way. They have no jurisdiction over us, our equipment
or our cargo. If we play their game, Reach 1779 won't be able

to land. Get the cargo ready to come off. I'll take care of things down here."

The loadmaster hesitated. "I'll be fine, Luau," she assured him. Her baby face disguised the fact that she wasn't easily intimidated. That she was on the small side in stature didn't help matters. "A little Texas charm, and they'll be eating out of my hand—or at least my glove."

That got a laugh out of him. "You got it, ma'am. I'll be ready for the green light."

And get that green light she would, Kat thought, turning toward the Virslanders as Luau loped away. While she wanted to backhand the officials for playing their ridiculous red-tape game while people were starving and freezing to death, people who needed the goods they'd brought in, she forced her half-frozen mouth into a pleasant smile. Long ago, she'd learned that body language was everything.

By now, flurries partially obscured the picturesque hills surrounding the airport. Visibility was on its way down.

She greeted the man who'd been yelling at Luau, figuring he was the alpha dog. "Good morning. I'm Captain Wallace, the aircraft commander. Thanks so much for your nice service here today. I'm confident the rest of the operation will go just as smoothly. I understand you have a concern about the cargo."

Only the man's eyes were visible under the fur of his hood as he observed her with definite condescension. Not unexpected, she thought. Women of authority weren't always accepted in these parts. "You bring unauthorized items to my country," he accused.

"Everything's listed on the manifest. Which particular items arc of concern?"

"The weapons are not there. We already looked."

"Weapons? No, no, these are relief supplies."

"We have report that you carry armament." His eyes narrowed. "*Reliable* report. You bring weapons to my country. To give rebels."

Her heart flip-flopped. Aghast, she observed the men standing with him. With rifles slung over their shoulders, they resembled thugs in parkas. Yet, they all wore airport badges that looked official. Nice group of folks running this humanitarian mission, she thought with sarcasm. "That report is in error," she said. "There's clothing and food. Medical supplies—"

"You come to terminal—all crew—make statement."

"Make" an interrogation, more likely, she thought. The accusations were outrageous. She could end the discussion now and return to the cockpit. They'd gang-start the engines and blast out of here, fully loaded. She'd hate to do that, but if it came down to protecting the plane and crew, she would. On the other hand, thousands of people were in need. Just because the Virsland welcoming party had turned delusional didn't mean the citizens should go hungry or cold.

The falling snow was sticking to the tarmac now. Her heart sank, seeing how it was also adhering to the surfaces of the plane. So much for her blast-and-go escape plan. Even the thinnest coating of frozen moisture could produce enough drag to prevent an aircraft from lifting off. She'd have to get the aircraft deiced before leaving. It was one rule you didn't mess with, unless you wanted to end up as a smoking hole at the end of a runway. Only the airport could provide the equipment to apply the heated liquid-chemicals. It wasn't a speedy process, either. It was just one more delay tacked onto the red-tape snafu fouling things up.

She needed the cargo off-loaded and the aircraft deiced or they wouldn't get out before the weather closed in. And Virsland wanted reassurance they weren't gun-running. Maybe, just maybe, if she got all the balls in the air at once, she might be able to make this work. "I can radio Morón and see if they'll allow permission for your inspector to look at some of the crates." And better yet convince these paranoid Virslanders that she and her crew weren't aiding rebels. "In exchange, I want deicing equipment in place ASAP and ready to go when we close up."

"No! By order of People's Republic of Virsland, you will make statement in secure area."

"Sir—"

"In terminal—all crew must go now!"

"I don't have the authority to grant you that. We also don't have the time. I'm trying to help us both out. There's weather moving in, and we still have another aircraft to land after we leave. I'll get the cargo off the plane. Good? We'll put it on the ramp for you, and you can inspect it at your leisure."

"Cargo stays on plane!"

Calmly, firmly, she replied, "Then my crew stays with the cargo."

The alpha-thug blurted out something in Virs. The minions flanking him slid their gloved hands to their rifles. It was a deliberate move to remind her they were armed, and it worked. Adrenaline spiked, her stomach tightened, and if her heart thumped any harder it would bounce right out of her chest. Without knowing how itchy their trigger fingers were, she was reluctant to move or speak for fear she'd scare the thugs into using those semiautomatics.

A double *whoomph-whoomph* banged from the direction of the airplane, shattering the tense standoff. The thugs swung up their rifles. Kat dove to the ground. Gunfire cracked, first from afar, then in ear-shattering bursts from the weapons only feet from her head.

"Close it up! Close it up!" she screamed to Luau in the cargo bay, a wide open maw that left the entire jet vulnerable. He'd taken cover behind a crate, but she knew he heard her and saw her. "Close it up! Close it—*now.*" Sealing off the plane was the only way to protect it, the cargo, and most importantly the people inside.

Her Beretta was in her gloved hand, but she didn't recall pulling it from her holster. Keeping low to the ground, she swung

her head around—and came face-to-face with the muzzle of a
semiautomatic rifle. The thug aiming at her showed no emotion.
His face was entirely devoid of feeling. It was as if she were one
more administrative detail to dispense with. All the coldness that
was in the air poured into her gut. The scenery around her seemed
hyper-real as time slowed down. He was going to kill her.

A single, crisp shot ripped through the silence.

Kat waited for the impact of a bullet, the agonizing tearing of
flesh. Instead, the side of her attacker's head exploded like a ripe
tomato. He jerked, spinning on his toes before he fell to the
tarmac. His body convulsed and finally went still.

Oh, God, oh, God. Raw, cold air seared her lungs and snow
stung her eyes as she scanned the tops of the buildings, searching for the shooter. Someone had just saved her life. But who?

More gunfire—single shots, methodical and accurate—and
two more Virslanders fell down, dead. Trapped and scared, the
remaining Virslanders fired back in wild bursts. More gunfire
joined the din: different sound, different direction. These shots
came from the airplane, she realized. It sounded like a 9 mm.
Holy hell, now Luau was shooting, clearly trying to cover her.

The cargo ramp was still wide open. Why hadn't he closed
the ramp? For a panicked, angry second she thought the loadmaster had disobeyed her orders, motivated by misplaced
chivalry. Then she noticed the silence underlying the sound of
gunfire. A noisy auxiliary power unit, the APU, located in the
tailpipe of the C-17 supplied heat and power while they were on
the ground. Most of the time, Kat never heard the small engine's
characteristic screeching whine; she was so used to it that she
simply tuned it out. But she sure as hell noticed that it wasn't
running now. That was bad news, real bad. No APU meant no
power and no way to close the cargo door, start the engines or
heat the plane. The severe cold must have caused a compressor
stall in the APU. That would explain the banging. The anxious

thugs thought the backfires were gunshots—and reacted by shooting. Unbelievably, her own airplane had torched off this insane firefight.

The snipers continued to shoot and kill with terrifying accuracy. One by one the Virslanders were picked off until only the man who'd given her so much trouble remained. He jumped into the van and started it up. Two shots shattered the windshield and then he, too, was dead.

No more gunshots. The back of Kat's neck prickled. Somewhere high above the tarmac, she was centered in the scopes of high-powered rifles. The snipers. She couldn't see them, but she knew they were there, watching. The feeling was overwhelming. Were they playing with her cat-and-mouse style, wringing amusement out of torturing their prey, wanting to see her sweat, maybe even beg for mercy before they blew her brains out, too?

"Come on, Captain—*come on!*" Tombo's voice bellowed from the cargo bay. "Get inside!"

The copilot's urgency shattered the shock that gripped her, the sense of time-distortion and unreality. Shivering, Kat pushed up to her hands and knees. She was so cold that she was stiff. Her skin felt frozen and numb where perspiration had turned to frost. The tarmac resembled a battlefield. There was blood splattered all around. *Not mine, not mine.* She was the only one left alive. By accident, or because they just hadn't gotten her yet? She wasn't waiting around to find out.

"Come on!" Luau was screaming along with Tombo now. "Get in, or I'm gonna come get ya."

"No, you stay put," she yelled back hoarsely. "That's an order, Sergeant." Her body quaking with adrenaline, she staggered to her feet, zigzagging as she lurched forward. Then, with the sound of her pounding heart thundering in her ears, she centered the plane in her sights and ran like hell.

Chapter 4

Kat staggered up the cargo ramp and into the cavernous bay. Many hands grabbed her, pulling deeper within the protection of the plane. Subzero air filled the cargo area. Moisture on the walls had already turned into frost. Then suddenly Rachel was hugging her, squeezing the air out of her. "Omigod. Omigod."

"Rache," Kat protested, mumbling against the taller woman's parka as she crushed her close. "Rache. Hey. I'm okay." She wasn't really. She wanted to clutch Mack's dog tags and sob. She wanted to thank heaven she didn't wet her pants because the fear was still so fresh she couldn't stop shaking. She wanted to howl her utter gratitude at whoever fired that shot and saved her life.

Finally, Rachel let her go. Her brown eyes shimmered with relief. Snowflakes had stuck to her glossy dark-brown hair and black spiky lashes. Even in this frozen air her skin was a flawless deep gold. She reminded Kat of an exotic ice princess. It was one of the things she loved best about Lieutenant Morales: the woman was drop-dead gorgeous but couldn't care less about that. She might come across as girlish at times, maybe too playful for a particular situation, but you never wanted to make the mistake of dismissing her as just another pretty face. "I thought you were going to die. I swear, Kat. If they shot you, if they even so much as scratched you, I was going to go after them myself." A switchblade glinted in her glove. She followed Kat's surprised gaze downward. "Yeah, illegal as hell. I grew up in East L.A., and I know how to use it."

Kat squeezed her shoulders. "No, Rache. You weren't going to go after anyone. No suicide missions, no Rambo stuff. We're gonna keep our heads level. And together we're gonna get out of this alive." Kat turned to the rest of the crew. "Let's get this ramp closed up."

"No power."

"What's the status of the APU?"

"It's dead," Rachel confirmed.

"I tried to start her up," Airman Chin said. "Wouldn't go. It drained what was left of the battery."

No juice at all. They had a completely dead airplane. Kat rubbed her gloves together and stomped her boots, trying to get blood flowing back into her numb toes. Without heat and electricity the C-17 was a subzero meat locker with wings. It had to be twenty below or more in the cargo bay. The cold had embedded itself in her bones. As long as she was shivering, she knew she was okay. It was harder and harder to tell if her shaking had to do with the firefight she'd just survived or the hypothermia her body was staving off. A subtle mental sluggishness that she'd begun to notice was a more worrisome symptom of her falling body temperature. Mental confusion was something she couldn't afford. A misstep could cost all of them their lives, not to mention the loss of a multi-million dollar airplane loaded to the gills with supplies people really needed. "Did we at least yell for help on every radio we have before while we still could?"

Tombo nodded. "I was in the middle of it when the battery crapped out. Reach 1779 heard us. They know we're on the ground and safe. Well, alive anyway. They'll relay the info back to Morón. Everyone and his brother will know what happened to us, if they don't already."

"Well, no one's b-brother is going to be able to land here now. Look at the w-weather." Steamer was shaking worse than Kat. His lips were pale, and his teeth were chattering loudly. Of the group, she and Steamer seemed to be suffering the most from the cold. Their parkas fit the poorest on their frames, allowing cold air to leak inside. It didn't help that the wind had picked up. The hills were completely obliterated by clouds. It was only midday but already getting dark.

Kat didn't want to think about how cold the night would be. If the hostiles didn't kill them, the weather might. "If we can't close the door, we need to build a barrier we can hide behind if we have to. Steamer, Luau, get those Kevlar panels off the cockpit floor and bring them here. We'll use them as shields." She stowed her pistol in her holster. "I've still got thirty rounds. What about you, Luau? I heard you shooting. Twenty-six, twenty-seven?"

He cleared his throat. "Uh, I'm empty."

"You pumped all your ammo into the tarmac?"

"I was covering you, ma'am. And I think I may have hit one of them," he said proudly.

"Great. Everyone wants to be a hero." And she just wanted to keep all of them alive. "Look, we want to do our best to protect each other and the plane, and keep the cargo safe, but we're not going to die trying. No one expects us to. Not for relief supplies. That means no more shooting at anyone unless it's a last act of desperation in self-defense. I hereby forbid any further fantasies of playing hero, or—" she frowned at Rachel "—Rambo. Am I clear?"

"Yes, ma'am," Rache said, louder than the others. The switch-blade glinted in her gloved hand. "We're gonna be cool. Real cool."

"Won't be hard for me to be c-cool, m-ma'am," Steamer said, shivering.

Kat grinned at his joke. Then her smile faded. If she didn't get him warm soon, he'd go fully hypothermic on her and die. "Our most immediate concern is keeping warm."

Tombo snorted. "How? There's not exactly a lot of firewood around."

"There is up in those hills," Rachel pointed out. "Nothing but forest everywhere you look."

"Going hiking, Rache? I'll wait for you."

"Nah, I'll stay here and get dinner ready. Cutting firewood is man's work."

"Dinner." He snorted again. "You're still dreaming, girl."

"We can always open the crates and look for food," Luau suggested before Kat had to tell her copilots to shut up. "Blankets," he said. "Canned food. Maybe even a heater. No water, probably."

"We can melt snow," Rachel suggested helpfully.

"Excellent ideas, all," Kat said. "Luau, go ahead and start going through the cargo—" A sudden roar of artillery fire dragged her attention outside. She dropped to her knees. *"Get down!"*

The crew ducked behind crates, anything they could find, as a convoy of trucks with giant tires and smaller vehicles that resembled Humvees raced across the desolate airport. A small army poured out of the vehicles and stormed into the terminal building and the control tower. Muffled bursts of automatic weapons fire came from inside. As if the horrible weather and accusations of arming rebels weren't enough, they were now smack in the middle of an airport takeover.

It was no amateur operation. Not even close. These soldiers, mercenaries, rebels—whatever they were—looked well-trained, coordinated and efficient. And dead-on accurate when it came to sniping. She hadn't forgotten that she owed her life to one of those guerilla's skills with a rifle. The impassive face of her almost-killer came back to haunt her with every slam of her heart.

Kat grabbed for Mack's dog tags. The feeling of thinking she was about to die wouldn't soon fade, nor would the giddy, disbelieving shock of realizing someone had saved her life. Someone out there. The thought burned inside her like a tiny flame, giving her hope that the rest of her rescuer's cohorts would be like-minded toward her and her crew. Now all she had to do was pray they didn't get caught in the crossfire.

Eventually, the fighting subsided into silence. The stress of waiting to see what happened next was worse than the deafening silence.

A fat-tired truck left the terminal building and sped toward them. The vehicle was filled to capacity with soldiers that resembled terrorists more than an organized, sanctioned fighting force. The Virsland Army it was not. Which might not be a bad thing, she reasoned.

The truck pulled to a sharp stop by the aircraft. A group of men jumped out. Scarves hid their faces from the nose down. One of the men gestured to the others who appeared to obey him without question. His body language told her he was in control. The leader, she decided. Circling a hand, he sent several men to surround the plane. To guard it or to make sure no one escaped?

Kat's heart beat hard and fast. For reassurance, she reached out to connect with her twin, pressing a glove to her chest until she felt the outline of the dog tags hidden under her flightsuit against her skin. Dead or not, she still relied on him. *Help me not be scared, Mack. Help me to think clearly and do the right thing.*

Help me to get home to Liam.

The leader strode with purpose to the bottom of the ramp. The black scarf he wore around his nose and mouth gave him a menacing appearance. It made her think of grainy Taliban videos and heads being lopped off hostages.

"Hello. We mean you no harm," the man called up to them in perfect, accented English. It made her skin tingle. Alek Barons had spoken with a similar lilt to his deep voice. "We are friends of the United States. We are known as the Brothers and Sisters of the Forest, and we fight for the freedom of the people of Virsland."

"The Brothers and Sisters? You've got to be kidding me," Kat muttered.

Rachel cast a confused glance in her direction. "Who?"

"The Brothers and Sisters of the Forest were Virsland's freedom fighters during the Nazi occupation. They disbanded after World War II. Now they're back?"

"We're accused of smuggling in arms for rebels," Rachel said. "Maybe we did, and they're the rebels."

"Rache, guns and missiles mixed in with canned tuna and wool mittens? Come on. That's crazy." Thing was, the deeper she got in this mess, the less she believed it.

"Uncle Sam's played secret Santa before."

"At the risk of our own crews?"

"Do we ever really know what's in all these boxes?"

It was a rhetorical question. Crews had no choice but to trust that what the manifest stated was true. But using the guise of a humanitarian mission to smuggle arms to rebels? It seemed so outrageous she couldn't wrap her mind around the possibility.

She stood, shoving her pistol in her holster. His gun was bigger than hers. So were his friends'. The last thing she wanted was to provoke him and his buddies into another shootout. "I'll go see what I can arrange about getting us out of here." She squinted at the falling snow. "I hope first thing in the morning isn't too optimistic." She started toward the gaping opening in the rear of the plane where the leader waited.

"Steamer?" Chin's voice rang out, urgent and scared.

"Steamer, wake up, man. Captain Wallace! Something's wrong with Steamer."

Kat wheeled around. The loadmaster was slumped over and unresponsive. As they'd sat hiding from shrapnel and stray bullets throughout the attack, Steamer had succumbed to hypothermia. "Chin, Luau, wake him up. I don't care how, just do it!"

The men jumped into action, trying to warm up the loadmaster by massaging his arms and legs. Steamer was going to die if he didn't get warm. Lifting her arms in the universal gesture of surrender, she addressed the masked man. "Hello. Do you have a medic? I have a crewmember who needs aid."

The rebel leader's head jerked up at her voice. His eyes were two slits above that black face-rag, peering at her with a sudden, focused intensity she could feel all the way from the top of the ramp.

"Do you have a medic?" she enunciated. "A doctor."

He continued to stare at her. Why wouldn't he answer? Steamer's condition, this man's eerie similarity to Alek and the frustration of knowing they'd be stranded overnight ignited her simmering anger. "Damn it, I have a crewmember suffering from hypothermia. He needs help. And so do the citizens in your country, if you haven't noticed. We've got boxes of food and medicine here, winter coats and bedding, donated by my government and other countries. We flew all night to get this stuff here. We put our lives at risk to help Virsland, and all you people do is shoot at us!"

"Kat," Tombo stage-whispered in warning. "Maybe you shouldn't—"

She silenced the pilot with a wave of her hand. She was seething, punch-drunk with worry, terror and the cold—and an unwelcome memory of Alek Barons. Her rapid breaths burst out in clouds of vapor. The fluffy lining of her hood tickled her forehead. She shoved it back and out of the way, revealing most of her face. Her lips and cheeks were so frozen they hardly moved. "Please, I need your help. We'll cooperate, just get us a medic. My sergeant will die if he's not treated soon."

The rebel had stood stock-still all through her rant, cradling his rifle in a curled arm. Only measured breaths of steam coming from his scarf told her he hadn't turned into a block of ice. His men appeared uneasy at his silence as they mumbled amongst themselves. He turned his head and said something harsh in his language that shut them up. Then he gestured to one of his cohorts, a man in a smoke-gray parka—the medic, she guessed—before turning back to her. "We did not shoot at you. Our enemies did—the enemies of the people of Virsland."

Every word he uttered shot warmth through her. She could almost believe it was indeed Alek Barons talking. *Alek is dead.* And she needed to stay focused on the mission, which was about all she *had* focused on the past year. She'd have been adrift otherwise, grieving for Mack, second-guessing the choices she'd made, thinking too hard on love and loss. Nothing, not even her air force career, felt quite right anymore. Strangely enough, it took being stranded to realize she was lost.

Focus, Kat. Her situation was where her mind needed to be.

"We are grateful for your generosity," he said. "To prove this is so, we offer you food, water, shelter and, yes, medical attention in return. To do that, we must board your plane."

Doubt flared anew, and she doused it. She was close to losing a crewmember to the cold. She ran the risk of losing them all if she didn't get real and cooperate with the rebels, or mercenaries, or whatever they were. If there ever was a damned-if-you-do, damned-if-you-don't scenario, this was it.

She stepped to the side. "Yes. Whatever you need."

"We will also assist in off-loading the cargo. We have the equipment necessary."

"Thank you." Finally, real cooperation.

The leader motioned to the others then paused, telling her in that smooth voice that conjured a million damn memories, "It would be best if you stow your weapons."

She made a deliberate show of putting her pistol in its holster. Turning, she told her crew, "You heard what he said. Put away your weapons. They're coming aboard."

Once the weapons were away, the rebels marched up the ramp and swarmed into the cargo with the same efficiency they'd demonstrated outside when taking control of the airport. Within seconds, the medic was examining Steamer with all the skill of a person experienced in battlefield triage. The leader, meanwhile, strode through the cargo area as if he knew exactly what he was looking for. She couldn't keep her eyes off him. He even walked like Alek—Alek with more confidence. There had always been something about Alek that broadcast he wasn't entirely sure of himself, despite his insufferable cockiness. It made her heart ache for him sometimes, which he would have hated had he known.

The leader pointed to one crate and another. "This one," he seemed to say in Virs, "And that one."

The rebels sliced open the webbing protecting the cargo. Then, with crowbars, they began popping open the selected crates.

Kat's jaw dropped. "Wait—what are you doing?"

"Taking my supplies. The rest will be distributed to the people in need of them. You have my word." He left her standing there, gaping at the unbelievable scene taking place in her cargo hold.

The panels on the chosen boxes fell open. Kat's eyes opened wide. She heard her crew swear and suck in their collective breath. It seemed at least a third of their so-called humanitarian supplies were in fact war supplies, from guns and ammo to rockets, even small vehicles. It seemed she was now officially an international arms smuggler.

Worse, she and her crew had been no more than unwitting mules in this operation. That stung. She'd dedicated her life to serving her country. Her twin had sacrificed his life for the same cause. To be treated in such a cavalier way was insulting. The least the government could have done was throw a few Ravens aboard, knowing that if intelligence leaked, as it indeed had, they'd have help. Not that Ravens would have done much good today except maybe intervening when she'd almost gotten her brains blown out. And maybe gotten themselves killed defending you. True. She might have dead bodies in her cargo hold now instead of one very cold loadmaster.

Of course, if those high up in the government felt that secrecy would save lives then Kat had to swallow it no matter how bitter it tasted. Throughout the history of warfare such decisions had been made. When she took her oath of office, she hadn't said the words: "Protect and defend the United States of America, but only if I always get to hear the full story."

Unless…the United States didn't know about the weapons. This could be the Germans' idea, or the Danes', or even the Swedes'. Any number of bordering countries had an interest in stability in this part of the world and strong motivation for keeping an uncooperative militaristic dictatorship gaining strength next door. Any or all of them could have decided to use the historic bad weather to disguise a massive transfer of arms.

Shocked and exhausted, Kat leaned against the cold metal wall of the fuselage. She was so deeply chilled that she wanted to lie down and go to sleep. The rational part of her knew it was dangerous, she might not ever wake up, but the temptation to give in was oh-so seductive. Only indignation kept her eyes open, boiling inside her gut like a small furnace as a stream of rebels transported the military gear off the plane. *Her* plane. Once outside, the items were loaded into trucks in the deepening, snowy gloom. What would the night bring?

So cold…

A hand landed on the wall to the right of her head, startling her to awareness. Kat blinked, swinging her gaze around to the rebel leader. Her shivering stopped at the sight of a pair of gray-green eyes focused on her. "Finally," he said, low and deep. "A chance to talk to you, Kathryn."

She jerked in surprise. He knew her name—her full given name that no one ever used. Except for one man. *Alek.*

Stop the slush-brain act, Kat. The little girl with an unrequited crush act. The resemblance is just an illusion exacerbated by the cold, and you need to be a captain.

Her heart slammed hard as his gloved hand came up and pulled his scarf down to his chin. "*Jah.* It's me."

"Alek…" Her voice was as raw as her shock. Between her frozen lips and her astonishment it took more than one try to form a whole sentence: "I thought you were dead."

His mouth curved wryly. "Me, too. More than once."

Miraculously, impossibly, Aleksas Barons had lived through the coup. Survival had come at a cost. Days of stubble shaded the chiseled planes of his jaw. A fresh bruise covered the swell of his left cheekbone. The rest of his injuries looked years old: at some point his nose had been broken, and his right brow was split by an old, raised scar that he didn't have in Del Rio, either. There, he'd been Euro-god perfection. Here, he was a battle-scarred fighter. A Brother of the Forest. He looked dangerous, self-assured, frightening and not at all like an aimless playboy who lived for fun and not much else.

"You look like hell," she said.

"If I'd known you were coming, I'd have cleaned up. Not so easy to do living in a truck, or in a bomb shelter, but for you, Kathryn, I would do it."

She snorted. Then her smile faded, reality returning. There was so much she wanted to ask him, so much she wondered if he'd share. After all, they had been, at one time, friends. "How on Earth did you escape execution? And what about your father?"

"He was not so lucky, Kathryn."

Seeing the grief spark in his eyes, she stopped herself from asking if he knew of his son's fate. Even though he'd never acknowledged the boy, he must have felt something toward his only child.

He shook his head. "More later. Not now."

"Then tell me what's happening. What's going on?"

"That will also take time. For now I will tell you that I am leading a rebellion to return the government of Virsland to its people. We are close to victory, so close, Kathryn. It has taken six years to reach this point. Six years of fighting for our freedom, consolidating power and support amongst my people and in the Virsland military itself. Six years of allowing the government to think my being alive is nothing but a rumor, a legend. My existence mere wishful thinking of the part of the population who must live under this traitor, this dictator with bloodstained hands." For a moment his eyes turned so cold she gave an involuntary shudder. "By week's end, I will reclaim what is mine— mine by destiny and by the people's wishes." His tone changed to one that was all at once war-weary and tender. "But for tonight, you will have my personal protection. After what happened today, I'll take no chances." His voice turned gruff. "I almost lost you. Before my eyes, I almost saw you killed. I wouldn't have known. I would have seen your body, and…" He paused as if overcome. Intensity radiated off him. His fist opened and closed as if he fought for control.

She, too, fought off the nightmarish image of that rifle pointed at her face and the feeling of near certainty that she was about to die. "One of your snipers saved me. I know my people didn't. It happened so fast, it—"

"I saved you. *I* did, Kathryn."

Her head jerked up. Alek saved her life. *Alek* did. How did you thank someone for something that huge? "Thank you…" The words seemed so inadequate. She reached for him, grazing his sleeve with her glove. He followed the movement with his eyes then his gaze slid back to her face. It was electric. If she'd thought the chemistry between them had weakened over the years, she was wrong. Her emotional response to seeing him alive after all this time swamped her. Learning his quick reactions and skill saved her life almost threw her into his arms to kiss the living day-lights out of him. Only self-discipline, the observation of her crew and the stranger Alek had become kept her rooted to the spot.

One of Alek's men called out to him in Virs. Like Alek, he was tall but more formidable in build. His black parka and hood gave a peek of high, Scandinavian cheekbones reddened by the cold air and vivid blue eyes that tilted up at the ends. It was as if a Viking warrior from centuries ago had come to life. Rachel stood several yards behind him, appearing concerned—and having every reason to be. By all appearances, it looked as if Alek had cornered Kat, trapping her against the wall. Her strong emotion could easily be construed as fear. Kat thought of Rachel's switch-blade and hoped she didn't take it out and use it. She shook her head at her copilot to let her know everything was okay.

Was it? Hell, no. But the danger had nothing to do with the rules of war and everything to do with the things Alek Barons made her wish for that were totally inappropriate, irresponsible and completely impossible. He was even more off-limits now than he'd been when they were stationed together as student and instructor. She was under attack on foreign soil in dangerous conditions, and Alek was helping himself to supplies that she wasn't sure were his to take. Yet, he did so with grim determina-tion, not with glee or greed, telling her that the arms did in fact belong to him.

In English, Alek answered his man without taking his eyes from Kat's. His no-one-matters-but-you gaze triggered the same butterflies it always had. "*Jah,* Vincent. Everything is all right. It's Kathryn."

The man called Vincent focused on her with sudden wary curiosity. Meanwhile, Rachel's brow shot up. *He knows you? Kat, who is this dude?* The questions burned in her dark eyes.

Just wait till you find out, Kat thought.

"Lieutenant Kathryn Wallace," Alek said. "No, it would be captain now, yes?"

"Yes."

As soon as Vincent heard her name, he frowned. It was obvious by his unhappy reaction that he felt protective toward his leader, and that Alek had told him something about her. But what? That her decision that day six years ago led to him leaving pilot training? That she'd pretty much accused him of being unfocused, spoiled and lazy? And that was just for starters.

Alek explained, "Vincent is my chief of security. He tells me we are not safe here and will leave as soon as the trucks are loaded. You and your crew will travel with us."

"Travel to where?"

"A nearby village under rebel control. The night will be spent in what is known as a safe house. 'Safe' being relative, of course. As you know, there are no guarantees in war."

War. The word drove home the magnitude of the situation she'd fallen into by coming here. The realization of what Alek himself intended to do hit even harder. He was days away from staging a full-blown coup. Days away from rocking the world with the news that he was alive and once again king. If he survived the effort. Mentally, she reeled back from the thought of anything happening to him.

Despite her shivering, sweat prickled her skin. *Don't let his situation distract you from your mission. Get the airplane and crew home safely.* "I've got to call my air base ASAP. We've been out of contact for hours. I need a radio. A telephone. Whatever you've got."

"Phone service is out. The radios in the sno-cats are inter-vehicle only. You can use the radios in the safe house, if the loyalists aren't jamming the frequencies."

"A better solution will be to get power on the plane for a few minutes. I can radio my base from the cockpit no problem. All we have to do is round up a power cart, juice 'er up and we're good to go."

"A new storm is forming that is breaking all barometric records. The temperature has dropped five degrees Celsius in the past half hour, and it will go down more before it is over. We cannot stay here."

"You're not done loading the trucks yet. We can't leave. Let me use the time we have left to find power."

Vincent broke in, and a tense, curt exchange followed.

Alek nodded and turned back to her. "Let me explain our situation," he said as Vincent glowered over his shoulder. The chief exhibited the no-nonsense confidence of someone in law enforcement. She'd bet he missed little and that he wouldn't hesitate to kill. Alek had made a good decision in appointing him to oversee security, she decided, even though the man seemed to despise her. "Vanhanen's lackeys fired on you and forced us to reveal our positions. Now, there's a good chance Vanhanen knows what happened here, too. We hoped to use the coming storm to our advantage as we have used the others, launching attacks on key positions all over Virsland while everyone focused on staying warm. But, we had to move too soon. Not all my forces are here yet. Not all the equipment is here yet. It leaves us vulnerable to attack. The longer we delay, the higher the danger we will be caught in a position of not being able to defend ourselves—or you."

It was almost enough to make a girl apologize for being shot at. "Our power generator, the APU, crapped out from the cold. It made a couple of sharp explosions that must have sounded like gunshots to those trigger-happy idiots. They fired then you fired.

That's what started all this." And caused a carefully planned out military attack to go awry, and possibly Alek's plans to overthrow a dictator. "If I can get assistance locating equipment to power up this plane, I'll make my radio call while you're still unloading. Let me try, at least. I won't cause a delay."

"Vincent will place one of his security team in the cockpit when you make contact. It is to see that you give no unnecessary details of our operation here."

Her focus jumped to Vincent. He listened with a hard expression. His responsibility was to keep his leader alive, the future leader of his country. She could hardly blame him for being concerned that she or her crewmembers might give away sensitive information, even accidentally, that could get them killed. And if she didn't agree to a rebel's presence in the cockpit? She wasn't going to get to make that radio call, that much was obvious. "You have my permission to station one of your people in the cockpit."

"Then you have my information to try to power your aircraft. Max will work with your mechanic to obtain the proper generator. If by the time we are finished unloading cargo you have not been successful, you will leave. No negotiation. No argument."

"Yes. You have my word. When it's time to leave, I'm all yours."

At that statement, his gaze flicked to hers and darkened. What a choice of words, she thought, her focus sliding to his mouth. His stare also dipped to her lips before returning to her eyes. The hunger to touch him, to kiss him, flooded her. How could she be this exasperated, this frightened, this angry and still be so attracted to him?

Outside, a blaze of headlights flashed in the dusk. The noisy convoy of vehicles churned over the snow to stop at the base of the ramp. Alek turned to Vincent. "Make room in the lead snocat for the Americans."

Nodding, the security chief took a step back—with no small

amount of reluctance, she noted. It was clear he didn't like leaving Alek alone with her. Why? Didn't he know Alek was the dangerous one? Never her.

Finally the man turned to walk away and almost bumped into Rachel. The pair exchanged a noticeable double-take before Vincent strode off to do his leader's bidding. Rachel smiled, following him with an appreciate gaze until he disappeared down the ramp.

After Airman Chin went off with Max, the rebel Alek chose to assist them in locating the equipment, she briefed Tombo, putting him in charge of communication. "I'll be up there as soon as I can. But if you get power first, make contact whether I'm there yet or not. Get word out we're on the ground waiting for the weather to break to get out of here. You're going to be watched by one of the rebels. Censored if you say too much. Be extremely vague about the details. We're safe, that's all they need to know, and that we'll contact them as soon as we have access to better radios. Do you understand?"

"Yes, ma'am." And he was off.

Alek issued more orders, this time in rapid-fire Virs. The men—and even a woman or two, Kat noticed—responded to his urgency. Outside, vehicles she surmised were the sno-cats waited. With thick, tank-tread tires, they appeared quite capable of navigating snow-clogged roads. Chugging massive clouds of steam, they idled in an orderly row next to where the rebels loaded the last of the cargo into trucks. Their efficiency startled her. The cargo hold was almost empty of both humanitarian supplies and the weapons. A wave of dismayed incredulity swept over her. Her country and others, financing a revolution—and she'd landed smack-dab in the middle of it, trapped here while a little boy's heart hung in the balance.

More, she was about to leave a C-17 sitting out on the ramp in the hands of a foreign nation. It was an expensive asset. Was she making the right decision? Trusting the right people? Or was her endless and often inexplicable belief in Alek causing her to put her career at risk all over again like she did six years ago in that USAF briefing room? Alek used to play at being a prince. Was he playing at being a revolutionary now?

She jerked her attention up as the sensation of being observed hit her. Alek had returned. Her heart sank. She'd never been able to hide her feelings from him. He'd seen the doubts play over her face.

The memory of their last, fateful encounter six years ago boomeranged between them. He walked up to her, leaning close. Too bad running away wasn't feasible, because it sure was tempting. "'You're not sure you're good enough,'" he said in a very quiet voice. "'You're not sure you can be the man they want you to be, so you work hard at making sure you're not. Then you do not have to worry about destroying anyone's expectations. Or failing them. Or disappointing them.' That was the last thing you said to me, Kathryn. Do you remember?"

Her cheeks went red-hot with embarrassment. God, he remembered every flippin' word. "Alek, I risked my career to give you a break you didn't really deserve, and you thanked me by blowing me off. I was upset with you. What did you expect me to say?"

"Nothing more," he said. "Nothing less."

Damn it, she didn't want him to agree. She wanted his hatred to validate her years of guilt. Just as much, she craved his forgiveness. "I admit, those were harsh words."

"True words, Kathryn. They changed me. It seems another lifetime, those days. I can hardly recall it. I think you still see me as I was then. A player, yes? A man who doesn't care about consequences. A boy, Kathryn."

A pause as he searched her face. This was where she was supposed to jump in and assure him that she saw how he'd grown and changed and that she was certain all this wasn't just another lark commenced without regard for consequences. This was where she was supposed to say she believed in him. That she trusted him. God, how she wanted to. Only, doing so would open the floodgates to so much more than he realized.

In the face of her silence, Alek's eyes turned as cool and flat as green glass. The excitement he'd revealed moments ago had vanished, along with his spirit of accommodation for her requests, leaving a war-weary leader in his place. A stranger.

"When it is time, Vincent will call for you, Captain Wallace. Whether or not you have communicated with your base, you will go with him. You and your crew will ride in the lead sno-cat. The ill man will ride with my medic in the third. At all times you will do as you are told. To question my orders is to jeopardize your safety. Do you understand?" Without waiting for her answer, he lifted his scarf over his mouth and nose and strode away.

With that, their roles and the rules of conduct crystallized. Civilian or not, like it or not, Alek was in charge. The rebels seemed to trust him. Why couldn't she?

Chapter 5

Rachel tracked Kat down the moment Alek departed. "Who the hell was that?"

"Alek. Aleksas Barons."

"The prince? He's alive? How?"

"I—I don't know. The conversation didn't get that far."

Rache observed her with wide, delighted eyes. "Omigod. You like him. You really like him. I thought I detected a little something when you mentioned him before."

"We were good friends, Rache." Kat hoped the noise of moving cargo masked the hushed conversation. "That's all."

"Too bad." Rachel winked. "If you only saw the way he looked at you, girl, you wouldn't be feeling so cold. If there's any privacy at all where we're going, you two should—"

"Act like professionals and work together toward getting us back home, Lieutenant Morales."

Rachel heaved a big sigh. "Ma'am, he's *Prince Alek.*"

"Thank you. That's exactly my point."

"Here's your chance to have a piece of him."

"No."

"Why the hell not?"

Kat started to reply and stopped. Her answer would be the same it always was. She didn't want a piece of Alek Barons. She wanted all of him.

Seething with too many emotions to name, Alek lowered his head into the wind as he strode away from the immense cargo plane. His boots hunted for traction on the snowy ground. It was so dry and cold that the snow shifted under his heels like fine powder. *"I thought you were dead."* Kathryn's words echoed hollowly. Indeed, he'd come close to meeting his maker more times than he cared to count, first during the coup then in the years since, leading the resistance, fighting with others like him who were determined to restore the monarchy in his homeland as well as his people's freedom and honor.

He headed for the convoy of sno-cats to check their condition even though he knew Vincent had already accomplished an inspection. No one would question his repeat look-see, however, not after the intelligence breakdown today. Someone was feeding the loyalists information. Who would betray them and still call themselves a Brother or Sister? He'd find out, and justice would be swift as it always was amongst the Brothers and Sisters. Zero-tolerance for traitors. Tonight, however, more than suspicions of sabotage or broken equipment kept him moving around the sno-cats. He sought the bracing effect of the air to help him regain his focus after Kathryn's unexpected appearance.

Kathryn was here. His little Hell-Kat. Here.

How? Cargo planes had been landing for weeks during the brief breaks in the weather, all flown by faceless, nameless pilots Alek rarely saw but appreciated their courage and self-sacrifice nonetheless. He had many countries and many individuals to honor and thank when he regained the throne, and he intended to spend the rest of his days doing so. Today, though, had started like so many others the past few months. Then *she* appeared— Kathryn Wallace—suddenly before him in the flesh. She'd come walking back into his life, having no idea of her role in who he was now. That her dressing down had turned into his epiphany.

The look in her eyes when she realized it was him was seared in his brain. Mixed in with her qualms about him and his intentions was a bright spark of relief and joy. Yes, joy. Seeing it, he'd nearly lost control of his emotions, something he'd held tight in an ironclad fist all these years. It had taken everything he had not to sink his fingers into those wild curls and pull her close. It was more than a fleeting hello kiss he'd wanted. Much more. Had he not been toughened by denial and self-discipline, he'd have kissed her the way he'd long dreamed of kissing her: hard with the hunger of too many years of pent-up desire. Desire *for her.*

Then he remembered it had never been that way with them. And it may never be, even now. A woman like her would not stay single for long. It had been years. Likely she was married and perhaps a mother to one or more children. He was fully prepared to respect her situation while cursing his timing. The years had changed both of them, certainly. There was a definite sadness about Kathryn when always she'd been a happy girl. Did someone break her heart? Was she trapped in an unhappy relationship?

He frowned as the blowing snow needled his face. It was not his place to break up a family, no matter what the situation, but, damn it, if God had any mercy for his pitiful soul, Kathryn would be free. Free to be his. Why bring them together again if she was not? Virsland folklore insisted everything happened for a reason. Her coming here had happened for a reason, too; he was sure of it—his unexpected, precious cargo…his little Hell-Kat.

"Hoy!" Mattias, his field commander, called out the rebel

greeting as he jogged past, slowing to grip Alek's hand, glove to glove. "We're almost there, sir," he said, the emotion of the moment shining in his eyes.

Alek nodded. "*Jah,* the final run." One last push into the capital then Virshagen, and the palace would be theirs. After all these years, the return to the heart of his country was upon him, upon them all.

With a salute, Mattias took off, loping over the snow toward the terminal. He and his unit would stay here, holding the airport until the main fighting force arrived with artillery, a blizzard roaring in on their heels. The airport might be Alek's as of this shining moment, as well as the country's main power plant, several nuclear facilities, and the other, secondary airport, being held for him by Virs military that had defected back to his side. But his control of the hard-won locations was by no means secure. He'd long since ceased taking anything for granted.

Dozens of others—Alek's closest staff and guards plus the Americans—would join him in the safe house to wait out the storm. Others would ensure the cargo was channeled to the people, bypassing the government stockpile where it would sit useless, snarled in red tape.

A group passed by, carrying the stretcher holding the man from Kathryn's crew who'd succumbed to the cold. A nod from Valter assured him he'd be okay. The doctor was well-experienced in treating injuries and illness caused by freezing temperatures. Alek thought of the young fighter who only a few days ago was sweating up a storm as the surgeon prepared to amputate frostbitten fingers. The appendages looked waxen to Alek's eyes, like doll's fingers. He and Valter had seen worse than frostbite the past few hellish years. Far worse.

Vincent joined up with him. "The Americans made contact with their base. Communication quality was extremely poor but they were able to get enough words out to clarify their situation. And without clarifying ours," Vincent added with a frown.

"She knows better to put us in danger."

"I hope she uses the same good judgment with you."

"Meaning?"

"Distraction kills."

"You issued the same warning when I went in search of my son."

Vincent let out a wry laugh. "So I did."

"And I'm still here, *jah?* Living and breathing." Vincent was his closest friend. They were like brothers. They had each other's backs. But who had put the man in charge of guarding Alek's heart?

Rounding the last vehicle in the convoy, Alek strode to the lead sno-cat. The cargo crew was already boarding. In typical Kathryn fashion, she waited in the freezing cold to let her crew climb inside first. There was one other female, already onboard, and three males, all of them sturdy and strong. What was wrong with these men that they didn't insist she take shelter before they did? She was their commanding officer, true, but she was suffering far more from the cold than they were. Something inside him twisted, seeing her small frame lost inside the over-sized parka—which he'd replace first thing. A few curls slipped out from under her hood and blew in the wind. Her nose was too pink and her lips too pale. He wanted to pull her close, tucking her in his arms to warm her and hold her the way she deserved to be warmed and held. Always the tough one, she was. That strength only intensified his desire to protect her, to take care of her. If she only knew how he'd dreamed of her sweet surrender as he made love to her. He'd make her feel what no man had ever made her feel. A night with him, and she'd never want another lover. He'd make sure of it. She'd be his.

Despite the harsh conditions, his body reacted to thoughts of them together, hot, naked skin, a soft bed, hours to do nothing but focus on each other. Bliss. Not this hell. Not this hell of these past six years. Damn it, if she wasn't free, he'd…

No—no more guessing. He'd find out now. Right now. His

people cleared a path for him, stopping to stare as he tromped past. He ignored Vincent's expression of concern as he closed on Kathryn. She'd grabbed the rails, ready to pull up into the vehicle. Alek stopped her with a hand on her arm.

Her blue eyes were opened wide, as if she were afraid of what he'd say. They'd parted on tense terms moments ago, but there was no time to delve into that now. "Are you married?"

"What? No."

"Engaged?"

She blinked at him as if he were crazy. Maybe he was. "No."

"Committed? Promised?"

She shook her head. "No."

Then he remembered how frozen she was. "Board," he said, perhaps a little more harshly than he'd intended.

Her eyes darkened. Expelling an angry huff of air, she pulled herself up the stairs.

Alek hung onto the boarding ladder until she'd disappeared inside. It took all he had not to let out a rebel yell. Kathryn was free. Free! For a brief moment he almost forgot about the cold and the war, and the aches and pains of his wounds, both old and new, internal and external. For when it came to winning Kathryn Wallace's heart, he still had a fighting chance. He would not let the gorgeous Texan walk out of his life a second time.

A blast of warm air hit them as the sno-cat's door swung open. The sound of unzipping parkas filled the enclosed space as everyone crowded inside.

"Heat!" Rachel cried, throwing off her hood. "Oh, baby, that feels good."

The driver twisted around in his seat to watch them react to the warmth with his bright hazel eyes. "Thirty-thousand BTUs," he boasted in excellent English. "More than we need and all the heat you want." A blue scarf was twined around his neck. A fluff of light brown hair stuck up in all directions, alive with static electricity. He was young, really young. He wasn't even close to shaving yet. Was he old enough to drive? Kat wasn't sure what the rules were in Virsland, but he was just a kid. Yet a confident hand on the wheel told her he wasn't new to the job. What the hell was Alek doing, conscripting child-soldiers?

Tombo tugged off his wool cap. His ears went from pale and white to bright pink. "Bring on those BTUs. I'll take every one you got, driver."

Rachel was downright luxuriating in the warmth. Her cheeks were flushed from the heat although her eyelashes were still spiky from being moist with snow. Kat felt like a frozen little bunny in comparison. A head-to-toe block of ice.

"She busted his butt out of pilot training," Tombo informed Chin. Everyone was still digesting the news that the rebel leader was Alek Barons. Hell, she was still digesting it, too. "Now we're at his mercy."

Luau shook his big head. "Guess your mama forgot to tell you what goes around comes around, eh, Captain?"

"We're fine," she insisted. "It's all good." If only she could believe it. Alek sure seemed overjoyed to see her…until he sensed her distrust and withdrew, ordering her around only to track her down for what seemed like no other purpose than to interrogate her on her relationship history. He was alternately a new Alek and the old Alek and as unpredictable as he'd always been.

It's what you love about him.

Love. Hell. She'd keep that to herself. Having feelings for the man would complicate her life no less now than it would have back then. You do have feelings for the man. Yeah. *Acting* on them was what would complicate her life.

The cabin door opened and frigid air flooded the compartment. Vincent climbed onboard. He pulled off his hood and scarf, revealing eyes the color of blue ice, high cheekbones and straw

blond hair cropped short like Alek's. A vision of a Nordic warrior.
For a second time, his gaze caught on Rachel and lingered, an
admiring appraisal that Rachel matched just as boldly. His gaze
was slow to leave hers when he turned to address the crew. "As
some of you already know, I am Vincent. I serve as chief of
security for Alek Barons and his freedom forces. And this is
Tobias, our driver. A very good driver, some say."

"*All* say!" The boy flashed a grin over his shoulder.

Kat snorted silently. He was a cocky little thing.

"We must leave without further delay. A bad storm approaches.
At times we fight a three-way war: the Brothers and Sisters,
Vanhanen's loyalists and the weather. Sometimes the weather
wins."

"And then we win," Tobias chimed in. "The weather is on our
side."

Vincent lifted a brow, a wry, teasing glint in his eyes. "Is that so?"

"How else can you explain everything that's happened? All
our victories since this cold came. That coward Vanhanen hiding
in the palace, just waiting to be thrown out on his ass—I mean,
his bum." Tobias cast an embarrassed glance at Rachel and Kat,
and an apologetic one in Vincent's direction. "It's more than
luck. It always was. God is with us. I know it."

Vincent shook his head. "The optimism of a child."

"Hoy!" Alek climbed into the vehicle, immediately filling
the interior with his energy and magnetism. Time and tragedy
had not dampened his dynamism. In life, Alek Barons was like
a blazing torch in a room full of tea lights. No wonder every one
of the rebels seemed to worship him. You just couldn't help it,
just as she couldn't keep her eyes off him now.

He tossed back his hood and unzipped his parka. Instinctively, she found herself seeing if she could detect his scent, but
all she sniffed was motor oil and hot rubber. His cheeks looked
raw from the icy wind.

He bent to affectionately ruffle Tobias's hair before directing the boy's attention to a map displayed on the GPS. Tobias asked him a question in Virs but Alek responded in English. "No, I will not ride in the lead truck today. I wish to join our special guests."

Then the sno-cat lurched forward. Kat's heart leaped. They were underway in an adventure she never dreamed of with a man she'd long thought was dead, evading historic blizzards and a dictator's minions mere days before Christmas after she'd made a promise to her nephew and family that she'd been certain she'd be able to keep.

Several tank-like trucks led the convoy. Many more vehicles rumbled behind them. The mass of headlights arced across the deserted runways, aiming for a dark, thick wall of trees. Very faintly she could make out a narrow road puncturing the forest. Snow swirled in an almost white-out, seeming to wrap them in a cozy white blanket. The image was deceptive. It was deadly cold out there. The sno-cat's defrost system struggled to keep the windows clear. Frequent chunks of ice slid off and fell to the ground outside. Shivering, Kat couldn't imagine what kind of condition they'd be in if they had stayed on the plane. She'd made the right choice in this, at least. But would she be able to make the right decision regarding Alek?

She sank deeper into the seat, huddled in her parka. Heat lightning…muggy July afternoons…sun beating down on her skin… Conjuring visions of Texas summers, she did her best to warm herself from the inside.

Suddenly, Alek was crouched in front of her knees. "Take off your gloves."

"I told you, there's no wedding ring."

An amused glimmer in those silver-green eyes rewarded her teasing. "A ring, perhaps not. But frostbite? Gloves off."

She glanced around at the others. The cabin was noisy with conversation. She was glad to see her exhausted crew blowing off a bit of steam. Rachel was flirting up a storm with Vincent in-between elbowing Tombo who was likely teasing her with snide comments. Everyone had already stripped down to their flight-suits. She was the only one still wrapped in winter gear. She stared down at her hands. Let out a quick, self-deprecating laugh. "I don't think I can move."

Sighing, Alek shook his head. "Texas girls. Blood like water." Gently, he unzipped her parka, splitting it open and pushing it off her shoulders. Warm knuckles brushed her neck, just where her hair fell. Shivering, she wanted to close her eyes and savor the touch, even though she knew the caress was accidental.

It wasn't hard to imagine those strong, capable hands sliding up her arms, and curving behind her head to pull her close. She'd always wondered how he kissed, if he was as good as she imagined. Probably… Probably better than she was even capable of imagining, seeing that she hadn't a wealth of memorable lovers in her past on which to base any realistic fantasies with Alek. Her boyfriends had been nice but in the end utterly forgettable. It was probably some flaw in her, not them, that left her leaving bored and dissatisfied. That had to be the reason they'd never made her skin tingle and her heart race like Alek did.

He's a playboy, that's why, a world-renowned love-'em-and-leave-'em Romeo. This is what he does. He knows how to make women crazy. It has nothing to do with you, individually.

Aleksas Barons would have chemistry with a broomstick.

"Those captain's bars look good on you, Kathryn."

She felt the rumble of that voice in the pit of her stomach. "Thanks. You look good, too."

"Liar."

She yanked her focus back to his face.

"You said I looked like hell."

"I didn't mean you looked bad. You never do." She blushed like a teenager.

"Ah, so I look still good to you? What did you used to call me? A Euro-god."

Despite everything, she couldn't help letting out a soft laugh. Oh, how he used to be able to make her laugh in Del Rio. How long had it been since she'd last laughed like that, the kind of crazy, from-the-belly laughter Alek used to induce in her?

He bent his head, pulling off her gloves. Quietly, maybe even cautiously, he asked, "Will you make it a career?"

"I honestly don't know anymore. Ever since Mack died, I've been rethinking things. Rethinking my life. I'm my parents' last kid left. I'm not so eager to put my life on the line anymore."

"Mack is dead?" He sat up straighter, clearly disturbed by the news. It seemed to have hit him in the gut. Maybe because he'd become so familiar with tragedy himself the past few years. Experienced. "Your twin brother…"

"Yeah." She swallowed hard.

"When?"

"Last January. I still can't really wrap my mind around it. Mack was always with me, from my earliest memories. He was always there." Her throat closed, and she quickly looked down, making damn sure no tears came. She was on duty in dangerous conditions. It wasn't the time for sniffling.

"Kathryn, I am deeply sorry."

"I know," she whispered. Somehow, she kept from getting choked up.

He seemed to sense her struggle. "Let's see about these fingers."

Gloves removed, her bare hands were so pale they looked like a mannequin's hands. Alek's felt like hot metal as he grasped her fingers. She jerked away but he held on tight. It took a moment until she realized he was bending her fingers. They seemed too thick to move on their own.

Rachel leaned over her seat to watch. "Kat, why didn't you say it was this bad?"

"I didn't realize."

Well, it wasn't feeling so bad now, she thought as Alek started to massage blood back into her fingers. In fact, it felt pretty damn good. She tried and couldn't recall a time Alek had actually touched her after the day he'd kissed her hand at the lake. He did so now with such gentleness that it all at once put her at ease and made her hunger for more. "Mack left a little boy. Liam is six years old. He misses his father terribly and worries something will happen to me. I promised I'd be there Christmas morning with cookies from the North Pole." She smiled. "Cookies from Virsland. Getting shot at put a kink in those plans."

"Liam will receive his cookies," he said as if he meant it.

She perked up. "When will the airport be back in operation? The plane needs to be deiced before we can take off. And the runway will have to be plowed. If I can get a hold of a working radio or phone where we're going, I can work with the meteorologist and determine a take-off window."

"The airport is closed, and I will keep it closed. Usually reliable equipment falters in such deep cold. People, too. It will take days to dig out from this storm. I cannot and will not devote the time and manpower. I will find you another way home once we are in a safe location."

Hope leaked out of her. Of course, he had bigger things on his mind than just her plane and crew. This was a new Alek. There was a deep, inner self-confidence about him she found both frustrating—when it countered her wishes—and sexy as hell.

"How many are going to have to cut off?" Tobias called from the driver's seat. He'd removed his hat. Under his parka he wore a pair of blue overalls over a patched woolen sweater. It made him look even younger.

"Not sure yet," Alek called back. "Her fingers are pretty cold. Three or four, at least."

"Three or four?" Kat snorted. "Try none."

"Should I call Doc Valter?" Tobias reached for the radio.

Alek shook his head. "He's busy with Captain Wallace's other crewmember."

"Use my switchblade," Rachel offered, getting into the fun.

Kat tried to tug her hands from Alek's. He held on, a brow lifting in challenge. She had an image of those eyes, just as sparkling and mischievous, as she tumbled over a soft bed with him, their playful wrestling turning quickly into lovemaking. Her body reacted with a desperate flood of desire, to her dismay, and a flush of heated crimson in her cheeks. "I'm keeping every single one of my fingers, Tobias. No more medical diagnoses from either of you. Your leader needs to stick to leading, and you need to stick to driving." She smirked at Alek. "The kid's a total charmer."

"The girls seem to think so," he said wryly.

"How old is he, anyway? He seems really young."

"Thirteen. To be exact, thirteen years, eight months, and twenty…" He wrinkled his forehead then glanced at the date on his watch before he went back to massaging her hands. "Twenty-three days. Back-to-back skirmishes with Vanhanen's forces and two blizzards, it's been a while since I saw a calendar."

She coughed in surprise. Alek had never been one to remember numbers. His scores on pilot training exams attested to that. "Isn't that a little young to be a recruit?"

"Toby isn't a recruit." Alek paused. "He's my son."

Chapter 6

"Your son..." What a bombshell. She was stunned. "You found him."

"*Jah.* He's a good boy. A good son." Something wonderful and completely non-Alek glowed in his eyes—fatherly love. "I've done my best to raise him. It has not been easy when fighting a war, but I wanted him in my life. He will forever be in my life, Kathryn."

"He's adorable. And smart. You must be so proud. He's like a miniature you, with a huge spirit and an ego to match."

Alek laughed. "Ah, yes, a healthy ego. He is a Barons in that respect. But he is already stronger than I ever was. He experienced abandonment, death and hardship at an early age."

The remorse shadowing his face made her heart twist. "And love. He has you."

He kept his head bowed as he worked on her hands. "I want him to experience this fight, this war, so he understands the sacrifice we must make to lead our people. Only when I think it is appropriate do I allow him to participate—with my heart in my throat, trust me. This is a big adventure for him, more than I anticipated. He was supposed to be safely away before we moved on the airport. Instead, he witnessed the attack."

"There are no guarantees in war," she murmured.

"No. This is why most of the time he stays behind with Mary to work on his schooling." Saying the woman's name, he visibly softened.

Kat's heart curled up. Of course, Alek would have someone. When did he not? In the time she knew him, he was never alone. Well, good for him. He found someone here in Virsland. Someone who actually meant something to him. Alek had never gone for long with empty arms, or an empty bed, yet picturing him with this Mary bothered her the way the women in Del Rio never had. Was it because she'd always known the local arm-candy never stood a chance at winning Alek's heart? "I'm happy for you and Mary," she forced herself to say. "Is she your wife?"

"Ah, no. Mary is a dear friend."

"So, you're not married, engaged—" she tried to remember how he'd phrased it "—committed, promised, et cetera?"

That whisper of a smile again. "No to all. This fight for freedom is my wife, my lover." In a private tone so intimate it made her shiver, he added, "Though that is always open to change for the right woman." His gaze drank her in, leaving her a little breathless.

She glanced down at their joined hands. She didn't trust what she might say if she kept up that blazing eye contact. Alek was still single. He wasn't even sleeping with anyone, it sounded like. That was hard to believe. Maybe he meant since last week. That was more the Alek she knew. But the more she formed those thoughts, the more her common sense told her she was looking at a different man.

She risked another look at him—a longer, much more thoughtful look. His scars and bruises might be new to her but his mouth hadn't changed a bit. His lips were still as soft-looking, and as ready to curve into a smile or a laugh…or to give a kiss to any of the willing girls who used to flutter around him in true moth-to-flame fashion. He was definitely Alek Barons, but he sure as hell wasn't the same person she'd left in that briefing room six years ago. Whatever had happened during and after the coup, he'd went and gotten his son back. The old Alek had never mentioned the boy. This Alek was leading a rebellion. This Alek was a loving father. This Alek was older, more confident, less cocky and comfortable in his skin. This Alek was simply…

"Better?" he asked.

She blinked. "Better?"

Laughter sparkled in his eyes. "Your hands, Texas girl."

"Oh. Yes—they're better, much better. Thank you."

He reacted with a smug, satisfied smile. His effect on her wasn't lost on him. It never was, damn it.

And their handholding wasn't lost on Vincent. The security chief's piercing blue eyes paused only for a moment on their clasped hands before he glanced away with a frown.

She lowered her voice to a private tone. "What's up with Vincent? He keeps glaring at me."

"Ah. He knows my feelings for you."

Feelings. The interior of the sno-cat seemed to spin a little.

"He knows how your words changed me. That your reprimand turned into my epiphany." Alek's voice took on a raw and honest edge with that admission. "You accused me of being afraid."

She groaned. "If I could take back that day and those words, I would."

"If you did not say what you did, I wouldn't be here. I would have died the day of the coup, died a pitiful coward."

"You were never a coward, Alek. Never."

"But I was afraid. Then I embraced my fear. I used it to find my courage. See, courage is not the absence of fear but the triumph over it. The key to bravery isn't to deny one's fear but to conquer it."

She listened to him in awe. Clearly, he'd spent many a day thinking on this.

"That is what I learned the day I came home and saw my father die." His anguish frosted over into the cold glint of hatred. "I still see it, Kathryn," he confessed under his breath as the noise and conversation in the sno-cat spun around them, his proximity keeping them tucked in the eye of a storm—a storm of reunion after too long apart, of the tragedies they'd both experienced, of blurted-out words of reproof that turned into so much more than either of them ever imagined. And of a friendship that hadn't dimmed a bit in the intervening years and was crazily growing stronger with each passing minute. "At night in dreams. At first, nightmares came all the time. They visit less so now—now that I am fulfilling my promise to him. The last words he heard on this Earth were mine: 'I will win back our country,' I told him. I will do it in Haldor's name."

"Haldor. The first Barons."

"*Jah.* The first ruler of a unified Virsland…ten centuries ago."

She swore under her breath as the awfulness of what Alek had witnessed caught up to her. "You *saw* your father murdered."

"I watched Vanhanen put a gun to the back of his head and execute him." Alek's anguished, blood-throbbing grip on her hand kept her spellbound, as did the cold glint of hatred in his gaze. "I still see his blood at night in dreams. The nightmares visit less so now. Less so now that I am fulfilling my promise to my father."

Then the awfulness of what he'd told her sank in. "Your father was fighting cancer. Wasn't he still in chemotherapy?"

"*Jah.* A man dying of cancer and Vanhanen murdered him," he said in a quiet, deadly voice. "He was weakened, suffering.

He was at his wit's end with me and my behavior. He was in fact in the perfect position to be taken advantage of and he was. General Vanhanen didn't become our top military officer because he was stupid, Kathryn. He saw an opportunity and took it. And by God, I can't blame him. I didn't deserve to lead Virsland."

"You do now."

He let out a soft, weary laugh. "Six years too late."

"No. It's not too late. If the world didn't think you were the right man, other countries wouldn't be sending you supplies to finish the fight."

"I am the lesser of two evils. They don't want Vanhanen."

"Well, then you'll simply have to show them why they want you."

His eyes flashed with surprise then with pleasure so raw, so intense, that she felt the echoes all the way down to her cold little toes. "You have a way of cutting to the heart of an issue that always amazes me. I cannot believe you're here, Hell-Kat. I've missed our frank talks. I've missed you."

"I missed you, too."

His lips curved wryly. "And thought I was dead."

"The news said you were."

"Vanhanen would never admit otherwise."

"How the hell did you do it, Alek? How did you escape being killed?" What happened that terrible day she'd long wondered about, lying awake at nights fretting about?

"Good luck, a gift for athletics and God's good graces. Luckily, my martial arts classes were the only classes I ever paid much mind to. I managed to throw my body out of the way of the bullet Vanhanen fired in my direction." He let go with one hand to swipe it across his chest. "The bullet came so close it burned through my clothing and left a furrow across my sternum. Every day the scar reminds me of how close I came to dying."

"And then what? You were in the palace, surrounded. How did you get out?"

"I wrestled a gun from a guard, shot and killed him, which kept the others at bay. These were not Virs Raptors by any means. They were mercenaries. Their loyalty was with their wallets, not Vanhanen. By then, the bastard was cowering behind the throne. His cronies were either not loyal enough or not brave enough to fire at me. Or he thought he was smart not to have armed anyone else but his personal guards. At that point, I don't know if I cared if I escaped. I only wanted to hold my dying father. And I did. Until he took his last breath."

She saw how hard it was for Alek to talk about this part. He seemed to dig deep down to a well of strength and discipline. Her ability to talk about Mack was nowhere near as controlled, and Mack's death had occurred far from her sight.

"Then it hit me I was still breathing, still standing. In Virsland we believe everything happens for a reason. If I was still alive, it was because it was meant to be. I escaped down a rear balcony. The same vines I used to scale those walls as a boy. Then I simply disappeared into the chaos on the streets. No one recognized me, Kathryn. My clothes were in shreds. I looked like an addict, a ruffian, certainly not a prince. For the first time in my life, I was where I'd wanted to be—unrecognizable. To be without my meddling staff. To be out of view of the paparazzi. It was a bittersweet victory." His gaze seemed to focus somewhere faraway as the memories returned. "In those first days, I was completely alone. I was running for my life, a wanted man and in some circles a hated man. I wanted to disappear from this earth. I even contemplated taking my life. I was fugitive in my own country. And your words kept returning to haunt me day and night. 'You're a born leader.' You told me that, but I saw myself as anything but. Then, some citizens reached out to me, helping me in secret, for to do so they risked their lives and mine. They

expected nothing in return but my promise that I'd get rid of
Vanhanen. I found I could give them hope. Then as Vincent and
the other Raptors rejoined me, looking to me to lead them, and
as I came to see the hope so many of the Virs people placed on
my shoulders *not* as a liability but as trust, I vowed to find within
myself the strength to be the man my people wanted me to be.
That you wanted me to be, Kathryn."

She almost cried at that, and she was so not a crier. "And then
you went to find your son."

He nodded. "I started making my way west to Dumar. It is a
village on the coast where I'd last heard Toby was being raised.
I didn't know for sure. I wasn't even certain of my own son's
whereabouts." Shame tightened his mouth. "It was almost un-
bearable, those days until I found him, not knowing if through
my irresponsibility, my selfishness, I'd lost him."

They both glanced over at Tobias, healthy and happy, seeming
so proud to be driving the sno-cat. "But you found him."

"*Jah.*" Alek's eyes reddened with emotion that he almost immediately blinked away. Taking a deep breath, he let go of her
hands, patting them affectionately. "Now it is time to return to
the present."

"Yes," she agreed. "It is."

Intercom chatter hissed suddenly over the steady noise of the
churning treads. Alek got up to walk to the front.

In wonder, Kathryn watched him go. Despite his royal blood,
it was obvious Alek saw himself as one of the people now, and
was raising his son, his heir, to be the same. From all that she'd
read and pondered in the years since the revolution, this was what
the Virs people wanted, and needed: a people's prince. No, a
people's king. If Alek won his war, he'd be the King of Virsland.
She, on the other hand, was a farm girl from simple roots. The
disparity sent her reeling back from any thoughts of forging a relationship with Alek beyond one, long delayed night of passion—

if she had the guts to do even that. Or the right, she reminded herself. She had a mission to worry about, a crew to protect. Get everyone home safe. Then she could worry about herself.

And what she was going to do about Alek.

"I think I finally figured you out." Rachel plopped down next to her. "You won't take risks."

"I'm trying to keep us safe, that's why."

"You mean you're trying to keep *you* safe."

"I'm your commander. It's my duty to—"

"I'm not talking about the mission. It goes without saying you won't take chances with our safety. You're one of the best aircraft commanders out there—everyone knows that. But what about Alek? What are you going to do about *him?*"

Kat lowered her voice to a hiss, hoping to keep their conversation private. "We're traveling two different roads, Rache. It's always been that way."

"And now your roads have crossed—again. Cupid's whacking you two over the head with a two-by-four. I see the way you two look at each other. It's true love."

"More like a potential train wreck."

Rachel groaned. "Losing Mack was hard, real hard, I know. But you can't live the rest of your life expecting everything will turn sour in the end."

"I'm a realist."

"Being real means not being so cautious and so careful that you miss out on all the good stuff."

The good stuff, she thought. Like Alek.

"Guts, Kat. You've got them. Use them. Grab that brass ring, girl. Grab *him.*"

"Guts, Kat."

All of a sudden she was back in Peru, in a smoky bar in Lima with her friend Dallas Klein. The memory was a little foggy because the liquor had been flowing that night and Kat's grief was still so raw, but Dallas's words came back loud and clear. *"How did this happen?"* she'd asked Kat with her miss-nothing gaze.

"How did what happen?"

"You, flying a slow, fat-boy cargo plane. I can't figure out why you don't have an F-15 strapped to your ass." Dallas didn't beat around the bush.

Kat's answer was automatic. *"I don't need to be on the front lines."*

"But you'd like to be."

"My brother was already in a combat specialty. Losing both of us would devastate my parents. I didn't want to put them through that."

"All us soldiers worry about our loved ones, but for you it's an excuse to live your life according to other people's rules— rules you probably made up to rationalize being so damned careful all the time. Guts, Kat. You got more than you give yourself credit for. I've seen what you're made of in just a few weeks flying with you." Dallas had leaned forward then, her eyes intense. *"There's a saying: well-behaved women rarely make history. Make history, Kat. Something in you burns so brightly. Don't let the light go out."*

Problem was Kat's role as the younger twin, the quieter twin, was familiar and comfortable the way an old, many-times-washed pair of jeans were familiar and comfortable. It was easier to follow what others expected of her than her own heart, which sometimes urged her to fly off in wild, chancy new directions. Yet, all her life she'd sensed that just beyond her grasp was who she was meant to be, her destiny. The brass ring. All she had to do was reach out and take hold of it. But did she have the guts to do so?

Shouting from the front of the vehicle jolted her from her thoughts. "Halt, halt!" Alek was yelling into the radio in Virs to the other vehicles. The sno-cat's treads whined and shuddered into silence. "Lights out—now."

Instantly they were in darkness. All along the convoy head-lights extinguished. The entire line of vehicles was now invisible in the forest and snow. An ominous, flickering orange glow lit the road ahead, what she could see of it through the heavy snow. Heart pounding, Kat had her pistol out in record time—lots of practice today.

Everyone was on their feet, pulling on their hats and gloves and zipping their parkas. "The lead truck set off a landmine. There is damage to the vehicle but no serious injuries," Vincent said as Alek coordinated further.

"I thought the route to the safe house was known only to the Brothers and Sisters."

"One of our own has betrayed us. At the airport the loyalists knew about the arms. Now this. There has been a major breach of intelligence."

A breach of a breadth and depth that was not expected, she thought. Alek's actions tonight clearly demonstrated that. Despite his "there are no guarantees in war" remark, he'd felt the journey would be safe enough to allow his son to come along. He, too, hadn't counted on a traitor in his midst.

Alek slammed down the radio. He and Vincent suited up in their winter gear, checking their weapons with an efficiency that spoke of many other nights doing the same thing. He threw a scarf around his face. "The lead truck has numerous targets on the infrared."

"People?" she asked.

"No. Traitors," Vincent growled.

"And they will be dealt with accordingly." Alek's eyes were back to being shards of glass, cold and sharp. A gunshot rang out, distant, muffled. A volley answered almost immediately. "Down!" Alek and Vincent called out at the same time Kat did. Everyone hit the floor.

Tombo swore from behind a seat. "What the hell am I

supposed to do with a pocket knife?" It was closer to a hunting knife, but Kat could see his point.

Alek reached under the dash and tossed him a semi-automatic.

"Now we're talkin'," Tombo said.

"Do you know how to use it, Lieutenant?"

"I sure as hell plan on learning fast."

Alek ordered the group staring at him, including his son, "Keep doors locked. No one boards for any reason until you hear an all-clear signal." He opened the door. Snow gusted in with the most unimaginably cold air, so frigid that it froze whatever moisture it came in contact with instantly.

Outside the lead truck burned. It hit her that Alek was supposed to have been in that truck, but unbeknownst to the traitors, he'd decided he wanted Kat's company. Sickened by the thought she'd nearly lost him to a landmine, she watched helplessly as he leaped outside with Vincent. Alek Barons, leader of the rebellion and chief threat to Vanhanen's grip on power, planned to enter Virshagen within days. Vanhanen, clearly now informed of his existence, was pulling out all the stops to make sure that didn't happen.

Chapter 7

Numerous headlights flashed in the darkness: trucks, sno-cats, and assorted vehicles sturdy enough to make the journey. The rest of the convoy had caught up. Rebels spilled out from the vehicles and vanished in the blizzard toward the burning truck.

Tobias popped up from behind the dash to watch. His hazel eyes were wide with fear but a whole lot of wonder. She could almost hear the word "cool" forming on his lips. She reached for Tobias at the same time Luau did and shoved the boy flat. Toby's big adventure had turned dangerous and very real. Someone had ambushed them in the middle of the night, in the middle of a blizzard. She sure hoped Tobias was right about the weather being on their side. Trapped out here, they'd last only as long as their heat-providing diesel fuel.

She'd traded the airplane for a far more dangerous situation. *"There are no guarantees in war."* No, there weren't, but damn it, she hadn't signed up for *this* war, nor had her crew. It was Alek's war.

Her country had chosen sides, supplying arms for the rebellion, and from reading the news, she knew that most of Western Europe wanted Vanhanen booted out, too. That made it her war, too, didn't it? She wasn't an active combatant in this war until now, until Alek entrusted her cargo crew with protecting the very future of his country: his heir, Virsland's crown prince. If she'd denied being part of this war before, she couldn't say any longer that she wasn't involved. She was neck-deep involved, and so was her crew. A glance around the sno-cat's interior showed Rachel and Chin poised to use their knives on any potential attackers. She, Luau and Tombo had firearms ready to go. Protecting Alek's interests was protecting her aircraft and her crew. It kept her plane and her people of that lying sonofabitch Vanhanen's brutal clutches.

Her crew's actions tonight also showed young Toby who his country's allies were. Someday he'd rule this country—Russia's neighbor, as well as a potential Scandinavian financial powerhouse once the economy recovered. His future relationship with the United States might make a difference in a critical world event in the international arena. Like a pebble dropped in a pond, the butterfly effect, this could generate a much bigger effect in the future.

In that moment, everything seemed to change. With a sudden, deep sense of certainty and clarity, Kat knew that this way-outside-the-box and not to mention protocol alliance with Alek was the right thing to do. Even though her cargo plane crew was untrained in guerilla warfare, their assistance tonight would help Alek fight the loyalists and hopefully take back his country and his throne.

And, she hoped, keep him alive.

Outside, a small explosion like a grenade silenced the attackers, but only for a moment. The firefight continued. Alek was out there somewhere, putting his life on the line with no hesitation. For his fight. For his people. As if reacting to that very thought, Tobias tried to get up but she dragged him back down. "Let me up." The kid was fuming, obviously frustrated and humiliated. "Now."

"Absolutely not."

"But my dad's out there," he pleaded, distraught. Her blood pumped faster with their shared fear for his father. Alek would give his life to protect them, and they both knew it. "I'm not a baby. I can fight."

"I have no doubt you can. You're not just any soldier, though. You're the crown prince of your country. You're one of only two Barons left in the world, the very last of a thousand-year-old line of kings. You're all your father has left, Tobias. If anything ever happens to him…" She couldn't finish the sentence. God, if anything did happen to Alek… Kat swallowed hard. She swore that if she survived this—if Alek survived this—she was going to tell him how she felt. What she'd never stopped feeling since the day she first met him. "It means you've got to take extra care," she managed hoarsely. "You're not like the rest of us."

The boy absorbed that reminder first with a pout and then what seemed to be acceptance, and maybe even a flicker of pride. He gets it. He understands what he is. Either he was less fearful of failure than his father once was, or the influence of the man Alek was now had rubbed off on him. Kat suspected it was both. "It wasn't your choice to be born into this role, but you were. Remember who you are. Always remember."

His eyes shone he stared up at her, his handsome little chin cocked in determination. "I will."

Since when had she become advisor to a future king? *Since you developed feelings for this future king's father.*

After relentless volleys into the woods the rebels had finally silenced their attackers. A whistle pierced the hush. "That's the all-clear signal," Tobias said, sitting up. Everyone got up, holstering their weapons.

"Kathryn?"

"Yes, Tobias?"

"Thank you for the talk."

"You're quite welcome."

"Papa told me a lot of stories about you. Sometimes I wasn't sure if you were real or someone he made up to teach me lessons about stuff." He shrugged, adorably shy, his woolen hat tugged low over his eyes. "I could kind of tell you must have been real because of the way his face looks when he talks about you."

Uh oh. "I had to tell your father some things that weren't very easy to say. Or to hear," she explained a bit guiltily.

"That's what he said. He said you believed in him when no one else did. He said he was going to contact you when the war was over, but he wasn't sure if you'd be very happy to hear from him."

Her heart squeezed tight. "I would have been overjoyed."

"He's not like this around anyone else. He's in love with you or something. That's what Vincent thinks. He says you'll break my father's heart."

Well, that explained Vincent's attitude around her.

Tobias pinned her with a classic Barons stare, one elegant brow coming up. "But you won't."

"No. He's my friend, Tobias. I would never do anything to hurt him." If anyone's heart was in jeopardy, it was hers. It was why she'd never trusted Alek with it. She thought back to the days in Del Rio, the nights spent at the bars and hangouts, and Alek inviting her to slow dance with him, and all the times she turned him down, even after they'd become close friends. How she liked to pretend that her refusals were as hard on him as they were on her, and then laughing off the thought. After all, he was Prince Alek. But her instincts had been right; there had been something on his end, too: feelings well beyond basic attraction that she never dreamed they'd have the chance to explore further, without the limitations of student-instructor regulations.

"We're traveling two different roads, Rache. It's always been that way."

"And now your roads have crossed—again. Cupid's whacking you two over the head with a two-by-four."

Yeah. *Whack, whack.* She could feel the blows.

The rebels returned from the forest. In the dark with their scarves wrapped over their mouths and noses, their bodies bristling with weapons, they looked more like the bad guys than the good guys. They appeared confident, successful, yet everyone in the sno-cat waited with baited breath for a sign of Alek.

"There he is!" Tobias cheered with a heart-wrenching display of relief. His love and admiration for his father was so obvious. Seeing Alek through his son's eyes made her fall for the man even harder. The irresponsible playboy who'd so charmed and exasperated her had matured into a true hero strengthened by personal tragedy so horrific it was difficult to contemplate.

Alek pushed open the door, stomping his boots as snow showered off him. His eyes blazed with loving relief as he focused on his son, squeezing his shoulder, and then something else when his gaze swerved to her. Something that made her heart twist and her blood run hot.

Yet he remained outside the door in the raging storm, his expression turning stony. "We were attacked by loyalists. They are dead."

Just then a group of rebels carried bodies past the sno-cat. A single nod from Alek and the bundles were loaded into one of the vehicles. "Three less traitors to worry about," he explained, his eyes even darker now. Colder.

It was almost a white-out now, lending an eerie, mystical look to the scene. Kat squinted, snow flakes clumping on her eyelashes. Rachel made a soft sound of dismay. Tombo cleared his throat, and the others in her crew appeared downright uneasy.

They were soldiers, yes, but a cargo crew. Executions weren't everyday fare for them.

"It could have been you they were carrying back," Kat murmured. "Or Vincent. The thought will give me nightmares for the rest of my life."

"Then you will never let down your guard. Someday, when it is easy for us, you will be reminded of what it took to get there, and you will never cease to value what we enjoy, for it was hard won."

We? she thought. *Us?* He spoke as if he expected them to be together. To grow old together.

Her, a queen? A Texas farm girl? She fled the sheer idea of it.

"Guts, Kat. You've got them. Use them."

"Well-behaved women rarely make history. Make history, Kat."

Rachel and Dallas's voices chorused in her head. Two strong women offering unsolicited advice to another strong woman—strong in her professional life if not, until now, her personal life. Was this to be her destiny, then? Was Alek? Was a life with him and the potential to better the world the brass ring she was so afraid to grab?

"He's in love with you or something."

There had always been a part of her that held back from trusting him completely. Maybe, just maybe, it had been a safety barrier to keep him from swallowing her up, heart and soul. It was time for the barriers to come down. She wanted the good stuff. The brass ring. She wanted Alek.

After reversing course away from the potential of more land-mines, the convoy reversed course, climbing steeply on winding roads. They were no longer going to the village. With the intelligence breakdown, it was no longer safe there. Instead, they would seek shelter in the summer palace. "It is back under my control as of last night," Alek explained to her and her crew. "It is being protected and held by an army unit loyal to me.

Vanhanen's forces will not try to fight them in this weather. We are also fortunate to have a working radio there, where in the village safe house, we would not."

Yes, Kat thought. Communication.

"But it is not as close as the village. We won't be there until morning at the earliest. There is food aboard, and water—vodka, too, for a shot or two to warm the bones—and I suggest you sleep while you can." Kat scanned the sno-cat. It was crowded, but there was space here and there on the floor.

Outside, there was nothing but whirling snow. Summer palaces were built up in the mountains where it was cool. In the middle of the worst winter in history, staring down the worst storm ever recorded, they were about to hunker down in the coldest place in Virsland.

Kat woke many hours after falling into a deep, exhausted sleep. The vehicle was dim, quiet. Only a few were awake—the driver and the man assisting him. Kat was on the floor in the very rear where cargo would normally be carried. She felt downright snuggly. A blanket was under her butt and another thick wool blanket covered her. The firm pillow under her cheek was nice and warm.

The pillow under her cheek was Alek's chest. She pushed upright. Alek smiled down at her. "Good morning, Texas girl. Warm?"

She shoved her curls out of her eyes. "It's heaven, yes."

His voice was husky and low. It made it easy to imagine what it would be like waking in his arms in bed. "See? You would not be so cold living in Virsland."

It sounded like the beginning of a sales pitch. "Really?"

"Our summers here are mild."

"Is that so?"

"Barring this crazy weather, it only grows cold, truly cold, come Christmastime. After all, this is the land of Santa Claus and he requires snow to make his toys."

She smiled. "I never heard that."

"It is true. But, there are many ways to stay warm in our cold season."

She swallowed, her gaze falling to his mouth.

"Roaring fires. Local vodka. Warm furs…" His eyes flashed a familiar, mischievous sparkle as he held her close. "…warm arms."

"Warm lips…"

"Jah," he murmured. His hand ever so lightly came to rest on her cheek. His palm was warm and slightly rough. The stroking of his thumb over his jaw was hypnotic, his eyes shadowed and dark as he gazed down at her. He seemed to drink her in with those eyes. She was afraid to move and break the spell.

It was a spell, a miracle that they were even here, together. So many things could have changed the way events turned out tonight. He might have been killed by the landmine had she not been on this mission, or even if she'd been on that second C-17 that didn't get in. Then he'd have been riding in that truck instead of in the sno-cat with her. Instead, he was alive, and she was here, having just been told by his son that he was in love with her and seeing the proof of it in his eyes. She had a sudden sense of everything changing. Of her world flipping end over end.

I am afraid.

"Guts, Kat. You've got them. Use them."

"Something in you burns so brightly. Don't let the light go out."

Alek was a blazing torch in a world of tea lights. Coincidentally, Dallas had said something similar about her. The woman called her a bright light. Kat certainly didn't see herself that way. Alek does. Could it be that what attracted her to him also drew him to her?

What happened when two bright lights came together?

It was time she found out.

No one was watching them. The others were either asleep or at the wheel. The churning of snow under the treads was loud enough to mask hushed conversation.

"Sometimes I am afraid, too," she whispered. Closing her eyes, she leaned forward and touched her lips to his cheek. Soft, warm...

He inhaled sharply though his nose, turning a fraction of an inch. The move brought his lips brushing across hers.

They paused there, breathing hard. So close to a kiss. "Of what?" he asked.

"Of this," she whispered back. "Of what might happen if we kiss. Remember in Del Rio, you used to ask me to dance."

"You always said no."

"It about killed me to turn you down, but I did anyway."

His soft smile faded. "Why?"

"Because I was terrified."

"Of me? But—"

"I was terrified that if we ever touched, it would be like spontaneous combustion, and we wouldn't be able to stop." His focus sharpened. The heat inside her grew. "It was safer to keep you at arm's length physically and let our friendship develop and nothing more than that. It was the right thing to do. I mean, we couldn't be together. If we'd been more than friends and you had your review ride, what would we—"

"Those days are long in the past."

"Exactly my point." Her heart couldn't be beating any faster. She was more lightheaded and afraid than she'd been facing down the muzzle of that loyalist thug's gun. She curved one hand behind his neck and touched her lips to one side of his mouth. Then, as he seemed to hold his breath in surprise and pleasure, she pressed tiny, soft-as-a-whisper kisses across the seam of his lips.

"Kathryn," he breathed. "Ah, my little Hell-Kat..." His fingers slid into her hair at the base of her skull as he brought his lips to her forehead. She trembled. He'd hardly touched her, and she was already shaking. It was crazy. She knew it would be crazy. It made her more certain than ever that the decision never to be more than friends with him in Texas had been the right one. He hovered close, his lips barely touching her forehead, the seconds crawling by as her blood heated to the boiling point, then stifling a sigh as his lips traced a downward path along her hairline.

She looped her arms over his neck. He smelled wonderful: like leather, smoke and man. He kissed the curly strands of hair floating near her cheek. Her eyes closed. She wasn't quite breathing anymore; it was more like little pants, and they hadn't even done anything yet. She actually couldn't believe they were doing anything at all after so many years of wondering…of imagining. Alek was a charmer of the worst kind. He had the knack, the ability to captivate a woman. And he had thoroughly, irreversibly captivated her.

Alek took her head in both hands, his lips parting. This was what she'd wanted, she thought, closing her eyes. This was what she'd waited for.

The sno-cat lurched, throwing them back. Alek grabbed her to keep her from falling. He muttered a curse in Virs. "We have arrived."

Outside, a weak gray dawn was breaking. Without electricity, the summer palace looked like Snow White's castle. It was like going back in time several centuries, or even only five decades, hiding out from the Nazis on a dark, winter's night. The sense of history was palpable.

With a rueful smile, he touched his hand to the side of her face. "We will continue this discussion…later." He lifted a finger to his lips then pointed it at her as if blowing a kiss. It was a gesture the old Alek would make, but it came from a man who was very much changed.

She was still so turned on by the near-kiss that it made her clumsy in getting dressed. Finally, she managed to get suited up. She heard whispering now that the treads had quieted. Rachel's hair was loose and wild. Her rosy lips made Kat wonder if she'd been sharing clandestine kisses with Vincent. How could she like the man? He had the warmth of a rock. But maybe only with Kat. There was definite heat sizzling between the security chief and her co-pilot.

Soldiers loyal to Alek guarded the enormous iron gates that framed the grand entrance. Kat remembered from pouring over photos that the grounds were exquisitely manicured with flower gardens, and the paths paved with ancient stones. The gardens were planted by Alek's mother, an American, the books Kat had bought over the years claimed, with many species from her native Vermont. None of it was visible under the many feet of snow.

The altitude was high; Kat sensed the thin air. Flashlights crisscrossed in the snow as rebels converged on the shelter. Faintly, she could make out wood smoke being torn from several chimneys by gusting winds. Inside, through the palace windows, there was a soft amber glow. Firelight. Warmth.

Kat tried to summon thoughts of Dallas on a hot and humid summer afternoon before setting foot outside. Taking a deep breath, she jumped down from the vehicle, landing in deep powder. The snow was blowing sideways. Although she tried to disappear inside her parka, the biting air still managed to find bare skin and sear it. The knee-high snow wedged between the top of her boots and her pants. She winced at the ice heading south. Her eyes were tearing, the tears freezing on her cheeks, and her lips were stinging. She hated the cold. Hated it. How did the Virslanders live this way?

"Roaring fires...local vodka...warm furs...warm arms..."

And warm lips.

Suddenly not as cold, she hunted down Sergeant Clamm who she hadn't seen since leaving the airport. All on his own, he stepped down from his sno-cat. "It's good to see you walking around, Steamer," she said. "How are you feeling?"

"Fine, ma'am." He gave her a thumbs-up. "But you still look pretty cold."

Something bumped into her from behind. "Inside, captain," Vincent said, taking her by the arm. "Alek's orders."

"But I—"

"*Jah, jah,* he said you'd argue." The Viking steered her toward the entrance and marched her through it. "Go. He waits for you. For six years, he's waited for you."

She planted her heels in the snow just as he tried to push her through the door. "You can stop worrying. I won't break his heart."

His piercing blue gaze dropped to hers. He seemed startled by her words.

"His focus is Virsland," she continued. "No matter what happens between us, I won't and will not ever come between him and his country." She yanked her arm from his grip. "So you can stop being such an ass." She walked away.

"Kathryn," he called.

She stopped, turning. "What now?"

"That is not appropriate language for a queen."

Her heart stopped. Alek's loyal guard and friend had just thrown out a peace offering, albeit a gruff one. His smile was slow in coming, but when she saw it appear, she returned it. They'd reached an understanding of sorts. In his way, he'd accepted her, or at least had started down that path. She still sensed his reservations, but that was understandable. It was his job to look out for Alek. All these years she'd been apart from Alek, Vincent had been there, serving as protector and friend.

"Oh, Vincent. One more thing."

He waited, snow coating his fur lined hood.

"Well-behaved women rarely make history." She paused to let the words sink in before she winked at him. Then, putting a little flounce in her step, she squared her shoulders and strode through inside the palace gates.

A blazing hearth dominated the grand foyer, bringing not quite enough warmth to the cavernous interior. Candlelight did little to ward off centuries' old shadows. There should be torches blazing instead, as they probably did in ancient days. But the early kings and queens of Virsland didn't need to worry about attacks with modern weaponry. Yet, the palace was airier and more delicate architecturally than she'd expected, a place meant for summertime not winter's chill. It wasn't hard to imagine the tall windows thrown open to allow in summer breezes, scented with flowers in the gardens.

Alek was deep in conversation with a bevy of men and women who appeared to be advisors. It had been a tense, eventful twenty-four hours, and their faces reflected that. Toby was already seated at a table spread with typical Virs country fare: herring, dark rye bread and cheese. Rebels and army personnel also helped themselves to the food. The rebel she recognized as Max, the man who'd helped power up the airplane, approached her with a plate of food. Others did the same for the rest of her crew. Despite the ambush and the executions, the rebels were high-spirited, boasting of their plans to enter the capital, Virshagen, in only a few days' time. Alek's war.

Her war, too. With each passing moment, she felt herself pulled deeper into his world. The past year mourning Mack had been far more difficult than she'd expected. But here, she felt alive again. She felt hope.

A couple of what appeared to be high-ranking military officers spoke with Alek next. Alek listened carefully and with interest. A leader. A *king*.

Kat looked around for the radio. She'd better get started trying to open a line of communication. Military equipment and boxes joined priceless antiques. There were a lot of weapons scattered around, as well as discarded coats and other winter gear like snow shoes and cross country skis. The air was scented with wood smoke and the aromas of cooking food—bread and something fishy, probably more herring, a Virslander staple. Here and there a few homemade wreaths and evergreen boughs had been put up in a touching attempt at holiday cheer. It was an urgent reminder that Christmas was fast approaching, and she was still far from home.

Near the hearth, she peeled off the worthless gloves and the worthless parka. She would have liked to throw it in the fire for all the good it had done her the past two days.

"Kathryn." Her heart swelling, she turned, expecting to see a broad smile on Alek's face. He appeared more serious than she'd seen him since the executions. Her stomach wobbled, but she squared her shoulders. "Bad news?" she asked calmly.

"*Jah.* Vanhanen's told your state department that rebels are holding you hostage."

"Damn it. I'll take care of this. Where's the radio?" By the time she was done talking there would be no doubt in any country in the free world that she and her cargo crew had been rescued by the rebels, not taken prisoner. One thing was certain: Vanhanen was going down.

Chapter 8

The situation worsened over the course of the day and into another night. From what they could discern from intermittent satellite television, there was almost universal international outrage at Vanhanen's lies, and demands to relinquish power.

Via a streaming video they managed to get out via intermittent Internet, Alek finally revealed his existence. He stunned the entire world—if not his own people. The Virslanders knew. They'd always known. With faith, they'd waited for his return. Soon. The day was fast approaching.

The United States, Germany and Sweden set up a blockade in the Baltic to put pressure on Vanhanen. Russia was demanding talks. Vanhanen was eerily silent. The longer the silence went on, the more Kat feared for Alek's life. The former general would not go out without a fight. He'd failed to kill Alek the first time. She was certain he wouldn't want to fail a second time.

The fast-moving storm had passed, but many feet of snow

covered the ground, making most travel impossible. Alek would have his work cut out for him getting to Virshagen. Vanhanen was counting on that, no doubt about it.

The world waited tensely as the future of a country hung in the balance. Danger was all around them, Christmas was fast approaching, and she was snowbound with a prince.

A prince who very soon would officially be crowned king.

The next afternoon, milky daylight illuminated the tall, frosted-over windows. The palace was designed for long, summer days—and nights—not winter. Yet, it was lovely nonetheless.

Alek had been gone for hours in meetings with his staff and, she presumed, communicating outside the summer palace when he could and with whom he could about the situation. In the quiet, shadowy dining room with a blazing fire in the hearth, Kat sat with her crew at the dining room table over a meal she didn't have the appetite to eat. She picked at a piece of rich, dark bread while Tombo played chess with Chin to pass the time. The wait to find out when or even if they were leaving, and how, was interminable.

Looking tired and pensive, Rachel rested her chin on the heel of her palm, her watchful gaze on the door. Waiting for Vincent, Kat knew, just as she waited for Alek, though trying not to be as obvious about it.

Luau was slumped in a chair. His hands rested on the tabletop, his head tipped back, snoring heartily in-between snorting awake with elbow jabs from Steamer. Their coffee was old, the tea cold. And still no sign on Alek.

"You've checked that door about a hundred times," Rachel told her.

"As much as you, Rache."

They shared a private smile.

"So, Kat, what are you going to do about him?"

"Ah, Alek." Her sweet Alek. Kat's cheeks warmed. "He's got a country to win back."

"And then…?"

And then… "We haven't really talked about it."

Rachel gave her an annoyed look and shook her head. "We have. Vincent and I."

Kat sat up. "You two talked about a future already? Wow."

"*The* future, anyway. If things go well here, I might try for an exchange program working with the raptors. I worked security before flying. It'd be a good fit."

Kat lowered her voice. "So will you and Vincent."

"He's…amazing. I've never felt this way with any guy before. It's new—we're new—but I'd like to give us a chance. To see where it goes." She cast a worried glance outside at the frosted windows where weak sunlight was trying to melt a small circle of visibility. "If we ever get out of here."

"We're going to get out, and you're going to be with Vincent. Have you ever let anything you wanted this badly slip through your fingers?"

"No." Rachel glowed. Kat had never seen her look so nervous, or so happy. Then, suddenly, she glanced up and her dark eyes danced. "Look who's here."

Kat spun around as Alek strode into the room with Vincent right behind him. Exhaustion shadowed Alek's eyes and lines of tension bracketed his mouth. Confident, in control, he looked very much a man of power. The spoiled, untested boy she knew in Del Rio was a distant memory. *This* was the potential she'd seen in him that day in the briefing room when she had to break the news of his failed checkride. This was why she did it, she realized. To get him to see and accept the Alek Barons he was meant to be. He was all that and more now. And sexy as hell because of it.

"Your rescue is underway, captain," he informed her.

Sharp relief mingled with an even sharper fear. She'd be leaving Alek to fight his war. Mack's dog tags slithered over her skin under her borrowed wool ribbed sweater, reminding her that not all soldiers returned. "When?"

"Tonight. Seventeen hundred hours."

"Six hours from now." Her pulse leaped again. She knew the term "hurry up and wait." This was more like "wait and hurry up." Now that it was happening, it was happening fast. She'd be ready.

Her crew was alert and focused on Alek as he briefed what he knew of the plan coordinated by several countries and led by the US. "They're sending in a Black Hawk over the Finnish border. There is a landing pad on the roof of the palace." Kat had a feeling only she noticed the slightest thickening in tone as he said, "My father had it built after my mother died. If he'd been able to get her to the hospital quicker after she fell we might have been able to save her."

"Then he'll be happy we're putting it to good use now."

His lips compressed as he nodded at her. "I need you and your crew ready to move out. I want no delays."

"You won't have any. We're as eager to leave as you are to get rid of us." They both knew that wasn't true. But it kept their intense feelings toward one another a secret. She wondered though just who they thought they were fooling.

After briefing her crew and ordering them to get some rest for what would likely be a long night ahead, she left the dining room. To her dismay, shortly after she'd begun briefing her crew, Alek vanished again. He'd seemed a little distracted, even worried. But when she exited the room, he was waiting in the hallway. He shut the door behind her, holding it closed with his hand. "No rest for you, Hell-Kat?"

He wanted her to rest? All she wanted was to be with him. "Alek, we haven't had a single minute to be alone together in the entire two days here—"

"And every single one of those minutes has felt like eternity."

His mouth came down over hers. A kiss. Finally, a kiss. Hungrily, she returned it. He made a soft groan of pure need, his hands closing around her upper arms. It was a mind-blowing embrace, as uninhibited as hell and way too hot for two people standing in the middle of a hallway used as a thoroughfare by revolutionaries.

Then, finally, Kat let her cheek fall against his chest as she struggled to drag air into her lungs.

Alek's heart thudded as loudly as hers. He lowered his head as his hand landed on the small of her back. A low, very familiar accented voice tickled her ear. "I want to hold you, my love. I want to touch you, every inch…" His hand slid over her knee and up her thigh, his thumb traveling along the inner side. He stopped before going any higher, locking dark and searching eyes with hers so there was no mistake as to where he wanted to touch her next. And what he wanted to do with her next. She was hot—on fire. His hand trembled as he seemed to sense how much she wanted him.

Seven years she'd wanted to be with this man, six of those believing he was dead and that she'd lost her chance. She was done waiting. If you waited, you lost. This might be all they ever had, and she would not let it slip away. "We need some privacy."

"We don't have a lot of time."

"We don't need that much, do we?"

I want all the time in the world with you, dear Kathryn, Alek thought, snatching her hand. *I want a lifetime.*

He pulled her away from the dining room and deeper into the palace he knew by heart. It had been at least eight years since he'd last visited. Aside from dust and dust covers, it was the same. Nothing like returning to a place that remains unchanged to find the ways in which you yourself have changed.

Silent, anticipating what was to come, he led Kathryn up a rear staircase. The private stairs. The family's stairs. It was warmer on the second floor but still cold. The empty hallways and bedrooms were filled with echoes and shadows of the past, a happy past. It gave the place a sense of being poised for a family's laughter to return. As first-born, he'd always known this would be his someday. Even though he'd never seriously given thought to staying with any one woman until Kathryn, he knew that someday he'd raise a family here. He knew that his children would run through the fields and climb the trees of the estate. They'd swim in the lake and lie on their backs at night as he did and count the stars. He'd taken many a meandering path, certainly many a wrong path, and yet this place had waited for him.

Waited for him? Was he mad? No matter how rosy he'd like to paint the future, unless he and his freedom fighters were successful, Vanhanen would continue to control this and his other homes. Not his family.

"My mother loved it here," he told Kathryn. "I think if she had the choice, she'd have lived here year round. Perhaps it's why this is the one palace that always felt like home. It's the one I always wanted to return to, even when I couldn't seem to run fast enough from who I was, and what I was."

Kathryn's warm fingers tightened over his. "The running is over now. You're home."

He wanted to spin her into his arms for another incredible kiss, but the sense of fleeting time was powerful motivator to find that privacy they both so desperately craved. He counted bedroom doors and found the one he wanted. "It's beautiful," Kathryn breathed, turning in a circle to take it all in. A southwest exposure had already melted a few holes in the glass. Long icicles hung, glittering outside the windows. Undisturbed, dust covers covered the various pieces of furniture and the bed. Evidence of damage and wear told him that Vanhanen's men had stayed downstairs in the main part of the palace and in some of the bedrooms. But not this one. He would not have to contend with the stench of his enemy to be with the woman he loved.

He walked around the room, throwing off the coverings and a good deal of dust. "You cannot tell for all the white, but this room has the prettiest view in the entire palace." Quieter, he said, "It is my wish that someday you can enjoy it with me as it was meant to be enjoyed."

"That's my wish, too, Alek."

Her smile was shy, and so sweet. His Hell-Kat. His Kathryn. He soaked in the sight of her face, heart-shaped with that plump, pink mouth he couldn't seem to stop thinking about, especially now that he'd tasted it. Her eyes, so blue, crinkled as she smiled up at him. Her hair, curly and wild no matter how hard she tried to tame it. Like her spirit, he thought.

"Even though I want to argue that I'm a Texas girl who never dreamed of this kind of life. Even though you're a prince—*a king*. I'm just a regular girl. A commoner."

"You couldn't be farther from regular or common. You're the most amazing woman I have ever met. You're the best thing that has ever happened to me. I'm the lucky one here. *I am*. I love you."

She shut her eyes for a moment, her lashes suddenly moist. Her eyes were so radiant when she once more opened them that it took his breath away. "I love you, too, Aleksas Barons."

He lifted Mack's dog tags from around her neck. With care, he laid the necklace next to the bed. "It's been six years since I've been with a woman."

"Six years? You mean weeks, right? Or months."

"I told the truth when I said this rebellion was my mistress. It's not that I didn't have the desire. Oh, I did hunger, many, many times, especially when I'd think of you. And perhaps, too, going without was a test of sorts. A test of my new discipline."

"A test, huh." She appeared worried. "Are you sure you want to break the fast, so to speak?"

"Yes. Beyond yes, Kathryn. Not even in the same universe yes. Can I make it any clearer?" He kissed away her laughter.

Then, lifting his head, he stroked his thumb across her chin and smiled. The light in her eyes made his heart do a somersault. Only she could conjure that sensation in him, from the moment he first saw her until now. "It's been so long I didn't even have any protection. You should have seen my frantic search. I was bound and determined to make love to you before you left."

"I thought you'd disappeared to another meeting."

"Instead I was tracking down Vincent and his little box. He was the only one I could trust not to announce my intentions to the entire palace."

Kathryn laughed, delighted. He swung her off her feet and laid her on the bed. They laughed and kissed as clothing fell away, their smiles soon fading in the heat of their passion. When he at last was inside her, he knew nothing had ever felt as right, or as good.

Urged on by her soft cries, he began to make love to her. He feared at first that he would not last long after waiting such a long time for this—for her. Maybe his body understood as he did that this might be their one and only time making love. Don't think of that. He pushed aside thoughts of war that tried to invade this moment and instead focused all his attention on the woman in his arms.

There was nothing frantic about their coming together, nothing rushed. Nothing awkward. It was a slow, intensely loving and affectionate dance. Deliberately, he kept their pace exquisitely lush, lavishing her with long, deep kisses and tender caresses, whispering his love for her and how good she made him feel. That he could make her tremble. He loved how she buried her fingers in his damp hair as she clung to him, and how she gripped him tightly, inside and out. And then, when he was certain he couldn't hold back any longer, she arched her back and cried out, a husky, soft sound.

She took him with her. He exploded inside her, his voice harsh and he said her name. "Kathryn…" She was still quivering as his own pleasure ripped through him. "My love…"

For the longest time he remained inside her, reluctant to leave her…in this and so other many ways. Then, they lied curled together, face to face, stomach to stomach, her legs wrapped around his hips. "I will hold this moment in my heart as I come into Virshagen. This moment will carry me through to the end."

She flattened her hand against his chest, over his beating heart. "You're coming back this time."

"You'll wait for me, Texas girl?"

Her expression gentled. "Until the end of time."

"As I will for you, sweet Kathryn. As I will for you…"

Chapter 9

Alek Barons strode through the wide halls of his ancestral palace of the Virs royal family. Trailed by freedom fighters, the Brothers and Sisters of the Forest, he paced with purpose toward the throne room. He could not believe what he had heard.

One hand crushed in a fist, the other gripping a pistol, he stormed past the walls of paintings in the Hall of Ancestors. Haldor watched him from the cracked oil painting, dressed as always in furs and armor, resplendent on his throne with his hounds at his boots. But this time he didn't glare back at Alek, daring him, challenging him to live up to his destiny. He was smiling.

It only added to Alek's impotent rage. "You find this damn funny, Haldor? That the pitiful excuse for a man who killed my father now lies dead—by his own hand?" As he bellowed, Vanhanen's body lay in the throne room, stinking of his own waste after the coward hung himself when it was clear Alek's takeover of the palace was imminent. The bullet Alek long envisioned putting through the general's head would never be. He'd never have that satisfaction now. Vanhanen took that from him. "What do you say to that, Haldor?"

The fighters with him appeared confused by his outburst. "A family issue," Vincent explained to them.

"I told you, boy, not to come back until you knew the difference between a life wasted and a life spent."

Alek went stock-still at the distinctive, rumbling voice of the ancient. A life wasted—his was wasted no more. A life spent—he was just beginning to understand. Over the past six years, he'd lived fully, meaningfully, giving back more than he got. He'd learned to be reliable, trustworthy, and brave. Learned to believe in himself. A life spent also meant not allowing his enemy's cowardly escape to ruin his moment of triumph. His people's moment of triumph. Yes, a life spent meant remembering why he was here in the first place. He was here for his people and his loved ones. They depended on him. Trusted him. He would never again breach that trust. They were who mattered, not Vanhanen's suicide.

He could sense Haldor smiling across the divide of the ages. *"Now you know the difference, and it will serve you well. Rule long and well, Aleksas. Long live the king."*

With tears of emotion filling his eyes, he turned, waiting for his son to catch up to him. He extended his hand to the boy. Toby caught it. Alek paused, savored. Then together they walked to the throne that destiny called theirs.

Chapter 10

The private jet carrying Aleksas Barons, King of Virsland, landed just after six a.m. Dallas time on Christmas morning. A private car sped him to where he knew Kathryn Wallace's family lived.

The farm was small and neat, and looked deserted at this early hour. A light in one of the front rooms told him someone was awake. He grabbed his two precious boxes and walked to the front door, rapping not-too loudly so as not to wake the little boy who lived here, if he was not already up seeing what Santa had brought.

He heard voices behind the thin door. "Who could it be?" they asked. "Who would be here so early?"

"Is it Santa?" a small boy's voice asked.

"Santa was here already, Liam."

He heard a gasp. Then, "Omigod, it's Alek!"

Alek grinned. Kathryn. His love. How he'd missed her.

The door opened and Kathryn flew into his arms. She smelled like bath powder and sweet shampoo. She smelled like heaven.

It was mass confusion of exclamations and introductions, and a good deal of laughter. He was pulled into the small living room with a gaily decorated Christmas tree as its centerpiece, pulled into the heart of a family that saw him not as a king, but as the man who loved their daughter, their sister-in-law, their aunt. There was so much genuine love here that he instantly regretted leaving Toby at home after they'd celebrated their own Christmas earlier that day. But his son had practically pushed him out the door, warning him not to screw things up. Later, Alek hoped to load Kathryn's entire family in the car after convincing them to spend the remainder of the holiday week in Virsland. He promised Toby he'd do his best. Next year, Alek vowed, they would all be together for the entire season. That was, if he didn't screw things up.

"I have something for you, Liam. Something very special. In fact, Santa himself asked me to bring it to you." He handed the wide-eyed boy one of the boxes. With reverence, Liam took it. "I flew all the way here from the North Pole so you would have it for Christmas."

Kathryn hung on to his arm as Liam tore open the package.

"Santa cookies! Real ones!" He showed them the box proudly and excitedly. "From Virsland."

Kathryn started to weep as she fell into his arms. "I love you so much, Alek."

"I'm glad, because I have something for you as well." He handed her the second, identical box.

Her brows lifted. "Santa cookies?"

"Why don't you see?"

Smiling, she lifted off the wrapping paper as her family looked on. "Santa cookies," she said.

"May I have one?"

Grinning and shaking her head, she opened the box. Her mouth fell open just as he'd hoped. "Alek…" She continued to stare. Well, it was an impressive ring at first glance.

He sighed, plucking the ring from the cookies. "I suppose this would go better if I got down on one knee."

Now her sister-in-law Kelly started to cry. A moment later both of Kat's parents were sniffling, even her father whom he had contacted in secret to request permission to marry his daughter. The crying was damned contagious Alek thought, feeling his own eyes grow moist.

He kneeled down on one knee, ignoring the numerous injuries left from years of fighting, and took Kathryn's shaking hand in his. "Kathryn Wallace, would you do me the honor of being my wife?"

Kathryn threw back her head and laughed with joy. "Yes, Alek. Yes."

Then he slipped the ring that his mother had worn, and her mother, and so on, onto the finger belonging to the love of his life. There would be Merry Christmases to come—many, many more, he hoped—but none quite as merry as this one.

* * * * *

Here is a sneak preview of
A STONE CREEK CHRISTMAS,
the latest in Linda Lael Miller's acclaimed
McKETTRICK *series.*

A lonely horse brought vet Olivia O'Ballivan to Tanner
Quinn's farm, but it's the rancher's love that might cause
her to stay.

A STONE CREEK CHRISTMAS
Available December 2008
from Silhouette Special Edition.

Tanner heard the rig roll in around sunset. Smiling, he wandered to the window. Watched as Olivia O'Ballivan climbed out of her Suburban, flung one defiant glance toward the house and started for the barn, the golden retriever trotting along behind her.

Taking his coat and hat down from the peg next to the back door, he put them on and went outside. He was used to being alone, even liked it, but keeping company with Doc O'Ballivan, bristly though she sometimes was, would provide a welcome diversion.

He gave her time to reach the horse Butterpie's stall, then walked into the barn.

The golden retriever came to greet him, all wagging tail and melting brown eyes, and he bent to stroke her soft, sturdy back. "Hey, there, dog," he said.

Sure enough, Olivia was in the stall, brushing Butterpie down and talking to her in a soft, soothing voice that touched something private inside Tanner and made him want to turn on one heel and beat it back to the house.

He'd be damned if he'd do it, though.

This was *his* ranch, *his* barn. Well-intentioned as she was, *Olivia* was the trespasser here, not him.

"She's still very upset," Olivia told him, without turning to look at him or slowing down with the brush.

Shiloh, always an easy horse to get along with, stood contentedly in his own stall, munching away on the feed Tanner had given him earlier. Butterpie, he noted, hadn't touched her supper as far as he could tell.

"Do you know anything at all about horses, Mr. Quinn?" Olivia asked.

He leaned against the stall door, the way he had the day before, and grinned. He'd practically been raised on horseback; he and Tessa had grown up on their grandmother's farm in the Texas hill country, after their folks divorced and went their separate ways, both of them too busy to bother with a couple of kids. "A few things," he said. "And I mean to call you Olivia, so you might as well return the favor and address me by my first name."

He watched as she took that in, dealt with it, decided on an approach. He'd have to wait and see what that turned out to be, but he didn't mind. It was a pleasure just watching Olivia O'Ballivan grooming a horse.

"All right, *Tanner,*" she said. "This barn is a disgrace. When are you going to have the roof fixed? If it snows again, the hay will get wet and probably mold…"

He chuckled, shifted a little. He'd have a crew out there the following Monday morning to replace the roof and shore up the walls—he'd made the arrangements over a week before—but he felt no particular compunction to explain that. He was enjoying her ire too much; it made her color rise and her hair fly when she turned her head, and the faster breathing made her perfect breasts go up and down in an enticing rhythm. "What makes you so sure I'm a greenhorn?" he asked mildly, still leaning on the gate.

At last she looked straight at him, but she didn't move from Butterpie's side. "Your hat, your boots—that fancy red truck you drive. I'll bet it's customized."

Tanner grinned. Adjusted his hat. "Are you telling me real cowboys don't drive red trucks?"

"There are lots of trucks around here," she said. "Some of them are red, and some of them are new. And *all* of them are splattered with mud or manure or both."

"Maybe I ought to put in a car wash, then," he teased. "Sounds like there's a market for one. Might be a good investment."

She softened, though not significantly, and spared him a cautious half smile, full of questions she probably wouldn't ask. "There's a good car wash in Indian Rock," she informed him. "People go there. It's only forty miles."

"Oh," he said with just a hint of mockery. "*Only* forty miles. Well, then. Guess I'd better dirty up my truck if I want to be taken seriously in these here parts. Scuff up my boots a bit, too, and maybe stomp on my hat a couple of times."

Her cheeks went a fetching shade of pink. "You are twisting what I said," she told him, brushing Butterpie again, her touch gentle but sure. "I meant…"

Tanner envied that little horse. Wished he had a furry hide, so he'd need brushing, too.

"You *meant* that I'm not a real cowboy," he said. "And you could be right. I've spent a lot of time on construction sites over the last few years, or in meetings where a hat and boots wouldn't be appropriate. Instead of digging out my old gear, once I decided to take this job, I just bought new."

"I bet you don't even *have* any old gear," she challenged, but she was smiling, albeit cautiously, as though she might withdraw into a disapproving frown at any second.

He took off his hat, extended it to her. "Here," he teased. "Rub that around in the muck until it suits you."

She laughed, and the sound—well, it caused a powerful and wholly unexpected shift inside him. Scared the hell out of him and, paradoxically, made him yearn to hear it again.

* * * * *

*Discover how this rugged rancher's wanderlust
is tamed in time for a merry Christmas, in
A STONE CREEK CHRISTMAS.
In stores December 2008.*

Silhouette®

SPECIAL EDITION™

FROM *NEW YORK TIMES* BESTSELLING AUTHOR

LINDA LAEL MILLER

A STONE CREEK CHRISTMAS

Veterinarian Olivia O'Ballivan finds the animals in Stone Creek playing Cupid between her and Tanner Quinn. Even Tanner's daughter, Sophie, is eager to play matchmaker. With everyone conspiring against them and the holiday season fast approaching, Tanner and Olivia may just get everything they want for Christmas after all!

*Available December 2008
wherever books are sold.*

Visit Silhouette Books at www.eHarlequin.com LLMNYTBPA

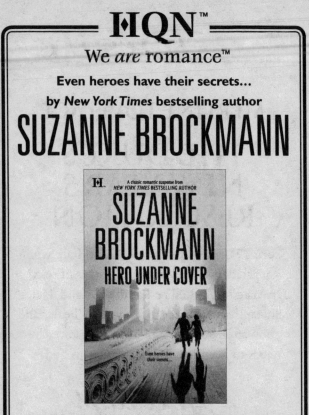

REQUEST YOUR FREE BOOKS!

2 FREE NOVELS PLUS 2 FREE GIFTS!

Silhouette® Romantic

SUSPENSE

Sparked by Danger, Fueled by Passion!

YES! Please send me 2 FREE Silhouette® Romantic Suspense novels and my 2 FREE gifts (gifts are worth about $10). After receiving them, if I don't wish to receive any more books, I can return the shipping statement marked "cancel." If I don't cancel, I will receive 4 brand-new novels every month and be billed just $4.24 per book in the U.S. or $4.99 per book in Canada, plus 25¢ shipping and handling per book plus applicable taxes, if any*. That's a savings of at least 15% off the cover price! I understand that accepting the 2 free books and gifts places me under no obligation to buy anything. I can always return a shipment and cancel at any time. Even if I never buy another book from Silhouette, the two free books and gifts are mine to keep forever.

240 SDN EEX6 340 SDN EEYJ

Name	(PLEASE PRINT)
Address	Apt. #
City	State/Prov.	Zip/Postal Code

Signature (if under 18, a parent or guardian must sign)

Mail to the **Silhouette Reader Service:**
IN U.S.A.: P.O. Box 1867, Buffalo, NY 14240-1867
IN CANADA: P.O. Box 609, Fort Erie, Ontario L2A 5X3

Not valid to current subscribers of Silhouette Romantic Suspense books.

Want to try two free books from another line?
Call 1-800-873-8635 or visit www.morefreebooks.com.

* Terms and prices subject to change without notice. N.Y. residents add applicable sales tax. Canadian residents will be charged applicable provincial taxes and GST. Offer not valid in Quebec. This offer is limited to one order per household. All orders subject to approval. Credit or debit balances in a customer's account(s) may be offset by any other outstanding balance owed by or to the customer. Please allow 4 to 6 weeks for delivery. Offer available while quantities last.

Your Privacy: Silhouette is committed to protecting your privacy. Our Privacy Policy is available online at www.eHarlequin.com or upon request from the Reader Service. From time to time we make our lists of customers available to reputable third parties who may have a product or service of interest to you. If you would prefer we not share your name and address, please check here. ☐

SRS08R

Silhouette®
Romantic
SUSPENSE

COMING NEXT MONTH

#1539 BACKSTREET HERO—Justine Davis
Redstone, Incorporated
When Redstone executive Lilith Mercer is nearly injured in two suspicious accidents, her boss calls in security expert Tony Alvera. But the street-tough, too-attractive *younger* agent is the last man Lilith wants protecting her as she faces her tarnished past. They get closer to the truth, and find that danger—and love—are hiding in plain sight.

#1540 SOLDIER'S SECRET CHILD—Caridad Piñeiro
The Coltons: Family First
They'd shared one night of passion eighteen years ago, but Macy Ward had never told anyone that Fisher Yates was the father of her son, T.J. Now Fisher is back in town, and when T.J. disappears, Macy turns to him for help. Will their search for their son reveal the passion they've been denying all these years?

#1541 MERRICK'S ELEVENTH HOUR—Wendy Rosnau
Spy Games
Adolf Merrick—code name Icis—has discovered a mole in the NSA Onyxx Agency, which has allowed his nemesis to stay one step ahead. In a plot to capture his enemy, Merrick kidnaps the man's wife—who mysteriously has his own dead wife's face! With the clock ticking and the stakes high, Merrick is in a race against time for the truth.

#1542 PROTECTED IN HIS ARMS—Suzanne McMinn
Haven
Amateur psychic Marysia O'Hurley figures her powers are the real deal when U.S. Marshal Gideon Brand enlists her help. The reluctant allies embark on a roller-coaster ride to rescue a little girl, with killers one step behind them. Even as they dodge bullets, will they find passion in each other's arms?

SRSCNMBPA1108

A